A PROBLEM FOR THE CHALET SCHOOL

Gr. 9

A PROBLEM FOR THE
CHALET SCHOOL

Elinor M. Brent-Dyer

Armada

For my God-Daughter, Elizabeth Anne Morgan
with all my love

First published in 1956 by W. & R. Chambers Ltd.,
London and Edinburgh.
First published in Armada in 1972 by
Fontana Paperbacks,
14 St. James's Place, London SW1A 1PS.

This impression 1982.

© Elinor M. Brent-Dyer

Printed by Love & Malcomson Ltd.,
Brighton Road, Redhill, Surrey.

"I KNOW I'LL HATE IT!"

"I'LL hate it. Oh, why ever did the Rector and Mrs. Gay want to give a scholarship for Miss Gay's old school? And why must they pitch on *me* for it?" Rosamund looked up piteously at Teacher, who gave her an encouraging smile.

"Hate it? Of course you won't hate it! Once you get there, you'll love it!" she said bracingly. "You're a very lucky girl, Rosamund, to have the chance to go to Switzerland and see all that beautiful scenery and learn to talk German and French. Don't talk nonsense!"

"But it *isn't* nonsense!" Rosamund cried. "I *shall* hate it! I wanted to go to the High School. But I won't know a soul in this place, and they'll all be looking down their noses at me because we live in a little house and Dad's a market gardener and Mum was a housemaid. At the High School I'd be with my own sort, but they're young ladies at that school!"

Miss Keatinge laughed. "Now you *are* talking nonsense. If they're ladies they'll do nothing of the kind—and Miss Gay wouldn't have gone to any school like that either," she added reflectively as she remembered some of the peculiarities of the Rector's daughter. "A school like that would never have kept her six years. Anyhow, you're the chosen one and your parents have accepted for you, so the next thing to do is to see about your outfit and uniform."

"Then that settles it," Rosamund said thankfully. "Mum and Dad can't afford to spend a whole lot extra on me like that, so I *can't* go. Thank you, Miss Keatinge, for all the trouble you've taken," she added, "Please thank the Canon and Mrs. Gay for me; but it can't be done."

"But my dear girl, your outfit, uniform and all, is included in the scholarship," Miss Keatinge said, looking with amused eyes at the flushed face. "So is pocket-money and travelling expenses. It covers everything." She swung round in her chair to face the girl squarely. "Rosamund, what *is* all this? Your mother told me you were always hankering after the High School. It was hard lines that you had measles when the exams took place, and that you were poorly for so long afterwards that you couldn't even be considered for the odd places later. Why are you making all this fuss about going to a place like the Chalet School, where you'll get just as good an education with travel in a foreign country and the chance to learn to speak foreign languages really fluently thrown in? In that last essay you wrote for me you said that your greatest ambition was to travel."

"I didn't mean *school*," Rosamund said, twisting her fingers together. "I meant being a lady courier or hostess on an aeroplane, or stewardess on a big steamer."

"But this would be the first step to that sort of career. If you can offer really fluent French and German you'll stand much more chance of getting a job with one of the big liners—air *or* sea."

"Shall I?" Rosamund asked doubtfully.

"Well, of course! That's only common sense." She stood up. "Talk it all over with your father and mother. The thing's settled and you're going after Easter. What you have to do is to make up your mind to it and be happy over it—and set to work to help getting your things ready. There isn't any too much time. The school goes back a fortnight after Easter and the day after to-morrow is Palm Sunday so you won't have more than three weeks at most. I know if I'd had the chance at your age I'd have leapt at it! Now that's all. Off you go home and let me see a more cheerful face when you come back on Monday morning. Good-bye, Rosamund."

Rosamund said no more. What was the use of saying? Miss Keatinge was very kind and nice, but she didn't *understand*. Well, you could hardly expect it. It wasn't as if she was *young*. To fourteen-year-old Rosamund, Miss Keatinge's thirty-two was a green old age. She said good-bye and left the room scowling fiercely.

Outside the school gates, she was met by Joan Baker who lived next door and with whom she was "friends", though there were things about Joan which had helped largely towards making Mr. and Mrs. Lilley finally decide to accept this scholarship for their youngest child.

Rosamund frowned blackly as Joan met her, exclaiming, "What an age you've been! What did old Black-beetles want?"

"Just to give me a message from Mrs. Gay," Rosamund said. "Decent of you to wait for me, Joanie."

"Well, of course I did. Is that all? What's Mrs. Gay want with you? Nosey, I call her! Had the cheek to tell Mum that she thought it a pity she let me and Pam run about the streets after dark. Sauce! What business is it of hers?"

In her indignation Joan nearly forgot her anxiety to know why Rosamund, who was generally the "good" girl of Standard VI, had been kept behind by Miss Keatinge. Nearly—but not quite! If ever anyone deserved to be called by the adjective "nosey", it was Miss Joan Baker. Her avid eyes searched Rosamund's face eagerly. "Go on, Ros! What's she want?"

"Just a message for Mum," Rosamund said. Not for worlds would she have told her startling news to anyone, least of all Joan Baker, until she had seen her parents. Besides, there was something in Rosamund that secretly revolted against Joan's assumption that there would be no secrets of any kind between them. She was very much under that young woman's thumb at the present moment, but that certain something had saved her so far from taking the worst of the harm this girl might have done her.

Joan was vexed. She tossed her head. "Oh, very well, then. I *was* going to tell you all about the larks Vic Coles and I got up to last evening, but if you're so high and mighty, it won't interest you. We went to the pictures and then we bought some fish and chips and went for a walk. We didn't half enjoy ourselves. Laugh! I could have died! But it's O.K. by me. Keep your silly secrets if that's how you feel. There's Kath Stevens! I'm off to tell *her*. *She* ain't a stuck-up bit of goods, sucking up to the Rector's wife and all! No; nor her Mum ain't fussing after her all the time. I don't know who you think you are, putting on all them airs. Your Mum was only a servant and mine was a young lady in a shop. But keep yourself *to* yourself if that's the way you feel. I couldn't care less!'"

With this final diatribe, she suddenly shot off across the road; but one ear was open for the call she confidently expected from Rosamund. If it came, she might go back to the other girl and after getting the whole story of the message from her, she might condescend to hint at certain things she and Vic Coles had said and done during their walk. That 'ud make the kid open her eyes.

Much to her surprise, Rosamund simply marched on without turning to see what was happening and Kath Stevens had already seen the girl who was the bane of more parents than the Lilleys and was waving to her eagerly. Joan decided to leave Ros Lilley to stew in her own juice. She'd come round by next day. Joan knew all about her own influence over girls of her own age and she exploited it to the limit. It was one reason why Mr. Lilley objected so strongly to her friendship with his own Rosamund. After he had found his girl in tears because Joan "was mad at her and wouldn't speak" more than once, he had been inclined to set his foot down on the whole thing.

His wife had stopped him because the Bakers were next-door neighbours and it didn't do to be at outs with such folk. But she, too, had done what she could to keep the friendship to school hours and Rosamund found a good many obstacles put in the way of her going off with Joan. But of late, especially since Joan had been going about with young Vic Coles who, at seventeen had an unsavoury reputation, Mr. Lilley had been saying that if nothing else would do, they had better try to get another house.

If it had been an ordinary day, Rosamund most likely *would* have called after Joan. As it was, she was so much absorbed in the awfulness into which kindly Miss Keatinge had plunged her, that she didn't care if she never saw Joan again. She trudged home, storming at her fate.

Presently, Rosamund reached the road where she lived with its late nineteenth-century houses built when land was much cheaper than it is today, so that the narrow two-storey edifices had a long and equally narrow garden in front and another at the back. They had five bedrooms, counting the two attics, but no bathroom. The family still took their tubs in the scullery in a long zinc bath that hung from a couple of hooks during the day.

Mr. Lilley was proud of his garden. The border running down the narrow path to the door was filled with gay daffodils and polyanthuses and the round bed in the middle of the narrow lawn had a Dorothy Perkins rose trained into the shape of a basket. In the summer, passers-by leaned over the hedge to exclaim at the effect and even now, in late March it was out of the common. Normally, Rosamund would have paused to admire it, but today, she stumped up the path, went round the side of the house and in at the back door which led into the scullery. She heard her mother's voice through the closed door, so she flung it open and went in, all ready to burst out into lamentations and pleadings. Then she stopped short. Seated at the kitchen table which was laid for tea, was Mrs. Gay herself. Mum was at the head, just lifting the big Britannia metal teapot to fill the cups of which she was so proud—they had been her mother's wedding set and not one broken, even after all this time— and a pleasant smell of baking filled the kitchen.

Mrs. Gay turned slightly at the sound of the opening door. "Here she is herself!" she exclaimed. "Well, Rosamund, has Miss Keatinge told you?"

Brought up short, Rosamund could only mumble, "Yes."

Mrs. Lilley passed the cup she had filled to the Rector's wife and said, "Just in time for tea. We can talk it over before the boys come in. Quick now!"

Rosamund fled. But all the time she was hanging her cap and coat in the cupboard under the stairs and running up to the bedroom she shared with her grown-up sister, Charmian, washed hands and face and brushed her thick straight hair, she was muttering to herself. However, she dared not loiter. Mrs. Lilley had brought up every one of her five to habits of implicit obedience and Rosamund knew what to expect if she dallied upstairs. She was down in five minutes time, and slipping into her place at Mum's right hand.

Mrs. Gay smiled at her pleasantly as Mum handed her

a cup of milky tea and indicated the plate of smoking hot Leafy cake, saying, "Seeing I was baking, I thought we'd celebrate today's news with Leafy cake and just lucky I did, seeing Mrs. Gay's dropped in to make arrangements for taking you to London to buy your uniform and such. Take a piece, love, and have some damson jam."

Rosamund helped herself with a quiet, "Thank you." Mum was very strict about good manners.

"Well, Rosamund," the Rector's wife said when the girl was munching the cake, "I hope you're pleased over having won our scholarship. You'll love the Chalet School. And you'll be seeing new countries. You'll be living amongst the mountains, and you'll see the Swiss Alps and the lakes and the Jungfrau. You'll learn to ski and skate in winter and in summer you'll go with the rest on expeditions." She glanced at Mrs. Lilley and added with a laugh, "And, of course, she'll learn French and German and any other language she likes, Mrs. Lilley. By the time her schooldays are ended, she ought to be talking them fluently and whatever she may decide on as a career, foreign languages are always an asset."

"She talks of going for an air hostess," Mrs. Lilley said in her pleasant voice which was just faintly tinged with a Hampshire accent.

"Then languages are just what she needs. She'll get all those, for they talk English, French and German on different days throughout the term."

"What? Lessons and all?" Rosamund gasped, startled out of her sulks by this.

"Oh, yes; everything." Mrs. Gay laughed again. "How Tom used to rage about it at first! However, she soon picked up enough to manage and now she's quite fluent. So will you be by the end of a year."

Rosamund was silent, revolving this in her mind. Her mother glanced at her.

"She's too overcome for talk," she said apologetically to the Rector's wife. "She didn't know anything about it till today. Miss Keatinge said when she called yesterday that she was going to tell her this afternoon and she hasn't had time yet to take it in, I'll be bound. When she does, she'll be grateful enough—won't you, Rosamund?"

There was a warning note in her voice, and Rosamund suddenly woke up to the fact that she was not being polite and Mum would tell her all about it later.

"I—it's terribly good of you," she stammered shyly. Then truth would out. "But why did you choose *me*?"

"Because the Rector and I thought you were the girl who would profit most," Mrs. Gay told her briskly. "No use sending a shy mouse like Marlene Dixon or a girl like your young next-door neighbour or that other child she's so chummy with—what's her name?—Kathleen Stevens, isn't it? It lay between you and Pamela Johnson and the Johnsons are leaving here in a month's time. Mr. Johnson has got a move up," she went on, turning to Mrs. Lilley. "He's going to the head factory at Coventry. In any case, Mrs. Johnson tells me Pamela wants to go to a business college for shorthand and typing when she's fifteen and then get a job as soon as she's qualified. But if you want to try for an air hostess job, Rosamund, you'll have to be eighteen at least, so it all fits in nicely."

"Rosamund's a lucky girl," her mother said. "I'm sure we're all very grateful to you and the Canon, Mrs. Gay, and she means to do her best to show you what she feels."

"So long as she's happy and enjoys both work and play that's all we ask," Mrs. Gay said rather surprisingly. "No, no more tea, thank you, Mrs. Lilley. I've got to get back to the Rectory. But I've enjoyed this so much. I'm going to beg the recipe for that Leafy cake. It's luscious!" She turned to Rosamund. "Tomorrow, you are coming up to London with me to buy your uniform. It comes from the one shop—tunic, blazer, blouses, velvet evening frock, hat and big coat. I've arranged it all with your mother and I'm meeting you at the station for the nine-ten train, so mind you aren't late." She stood up. "Not much time to do everything in, I'm afraid, but we wanted you to begin with the summer term. Oh, and we must order your name-tapes at the same time. Everything has to be marked or Matron has plenty to say about it! Now I really must go. Walk with me to the gate, Rosamund."

Rosamund got up and followed Mrs. Gay through the narrow hall and out into the garden after that lady had said good-bye. They went down to the gate. Arrived there, Mrs. Gay paused with her hand on the latch.

"I want to tell you something, Rosamund. This scholarship is in the nature of a thank-offering."

Rosamund stared at her dumbly. What on earth did she mean? Mrs. Gay explained.

"This is for yourself, Rosamund. I know I can trust you not to talk about it among your chums. Two or three years ago, we were very poor people—poorer than your people are. The Chalet School was going to Switzerland that year and we had to tell Tom we couldn't afford to send her. She must finish at the English branch. Then, through the school, an old friend of the Rector's, Dean Herbert, offered him this living and everything was made possible. We said then that we'd like to send another girl to the school where our own had been so happy and done so well as a sign of our gratitude, but you'll understand we couldn't do it all at once. However, we can do it now, and we've chosen you. We hope that it may be the first step towards the career you want—air hostess, if you stick to that. Our girl was very happy indeed at the school and she wants a hand in this, too, and she is giving you your pocket-money and your bank balance—I'll explain all that tomorrow in the train. But we want to make it a real thank-offering and that partly depends on you."

"How?" Rosamund demanded as the lady stopped to look at her anxiously. She was very conscious of Joan coming along the road and staring hard.

"If you can accept this gift and not only make the best of it, but do it joyfully, it will be a much bigger thing. I know you will feel that we are taking you away from all you know and we're all conservative creatures at bottom and prefer to stick to the old ways. You'll be homesick at first—and I shouldn't think much of you if you weren't. But that will pass and you'll be happy—if you try. Will you, Rosamund? You needn't be afraid you won't have plenty of friends there before long. If you don't, it'll be your own fault. Chalet School girls are taught that it's what we are ourselves that matters. Do you understand?"

"I—I think so!" Rosamund gasped. Joan had drawn level with them and was still staring.

"Good! Then you'll meet me tomorrow at the station and we can talk again. Now I really must fly. Good-bye!" She went through the gate and was off with her long loping stride. Rosamund turned to go in. Whatever happened, she felt that she couldn't let Mrs. Gay down now. She was committed to the big change. More; she had promised to do her best in every way.

A disagreeable voice broke across her reverie. "Sucking up, just as I said!" Joan remarked over the hedge that divided the Baker garden from their own path. "O.K., Rosamund Lilley! But don't expect me to be pals with you again. I'll take up with Kath Stevens. She isn't ruled to death by a bossy Mum who think's she's someone when she never was anything but a blooming *servant*! You can whistle for all the secrets I'll tell *you*!"

Rosamund looked at her as she stood there, cheaply pretty with her hair untidy and rough, despite its "perm", her insolent glance, her loose mouth and impudent bearing. For once, Joan's unkindness failed to upset her. She simply gave her that one comprehending look and then turned and went in quietly to finish her tea.

Joan was left staring. She wondered what on earth Mrs. Gay had been saying to Rosamund Lilley to make her behave like this. Oh, well, it didn't matter. Young Ros would soon come round and be whining to her for her friendship again. In the meantime, there was Kath who was ever so much more fun in some ways.

And when Joan went in at last to find that her grandfather had come for the week-end and proposed to take her back with him on Monday till after Easter, she chuckled to herself. That would teach Ros Lilley a lesson. She'd be as meek as Moses by the time Joan got back and ready to tell Joan anything she wanted to know without much bother. Joan, wolfing down slices of bread and jam and cheap cake from the grocer's at the end of the road, fancied that she would have the whiphand all right for the rest of their time at school.

13

CHAPTER II

JOEY

JOEY MAYNARD sat by the sunny window of her bedroom and gave vent to a low chuckle of sheer joy. It was three weeks to the day since her fifth daughter had been born and though she had come home six days after the event, both of them being, to quote herself, on top of the world, it had been to bed.

There she had been kept for another two weeks and at the end of them she had been seething with discontent. Joey Maynard never had had any use for bed except during the night-hours. However, on the Sunday, Frank Peters had announced that she might sit up for tea that day and next day get up for a couple of hours in the morning and again at teatime.

She was only partly dressed under her long green house-frock, but her black pigtails were twisted up in their earphones and she had already announced her intention of dressing properly on the morrow.

"And after that," she informed Jack Maynard, "it won't be long before I'm in harness again. I'm as fit as ever I was and Cecil is a model of a baby, gaining regularly now and behaving like a little lady on all occasions. I'm sick of bed and I'm getting up, so I warn you!"

"These holidays have been an awful waste," she observed to her eldest daughter who came into the room just then with her mid-morning cup of milky coffee. "That for me? Thank you, sugarpie. I can just do with it."

Len handed her the cup and then bent down over the old cradle—strictly rockerless—to gloat over her new sister. "She's just sweet, Mamma! I always thought Felicity was the most precious pet we'd ever had, but Cecil really has something! And it's so awfully nice to have a *dark* baby for once. The twins are so fair and so is Mike; and Charles wasn't really *dark*. Anyhow, I don't remember him much as a baby. But Cecil is a complete change."

"She is, isn't she?" Joey agreed. "No; don't take her up now. Her next feed is due in half an hour and I'd just as soon she slept till then. Besides, don't you remember what I used to tell you when the twins were tiny? Very new babies oughtn't to be handled too much."

"I remember—though we didn't get much chance at them," Len said, leaving the cradle and coming to drop down on the windowseat beside her mother. "We were boarders at the Convent in Toronto then and the Sisters are dears, but they wouldn't let us come home much during term time and we only saw the twins now and then. I'm glad we've had so much of Cecil."

"And," Joey said, "La Sagesse was at one side of Toronto and The Blue Sisters were right away at the other. Here, you're next door and I expect Auntie Hilda will let you run over on Saturdays and Sundays to see us here. You'll be able to watch her growing." She sipped at her coffee and then asked, "Where are the others?"

"The boys are out in the garden, playing tip and run. The Coadjutor has taken the twins and Mike for their morning walk. Margot is trying to finish her holiday task and Con——" Len stopped short and looked at her mother with deep violet-grey eyes that gleamed wickedly.

"Well? Go on! What mischief is Con up to *now*?"

"No mischief—not really. She's writing a new story."

"Oh, *no!*" Joey sat bolt upright in dismay. "Oh, my goodness! What possesses her to begin at this late date?"

"Oh, I guessed it was coming on," Len said calmly, hugging her knees. "She's been waffly for the past week."

"You might have warned me. I'd have done what in me lay to postpone it. Con up to the eyes in a new composition is no use to either man or beast. School opens on Thursday and she ought to be giving her mind to it then."

"I couldn't tell you. Papa said we weren't to say anything to worry you until you were up again," Len replied simply. "It'll be all right, Mamma. It's only a short. She'll have finished by the time we go back to school."

"Let's hope and pray it runs well and she really does finish by Wednesday night! Otherwise, I see her getting into all sorts of trouble over her lessons."

"She won't," Len said confidently. "She's never been

so bad since last year when she made that awful howler about Daniel in the lions' den."[1]

She stopped there and mother and daughter giggled. Con, the second of the triplets, had contrived to add to the legends of the Chalet School on that occasion.

"Let's hope that memory holds good," Joey said. Then she paused and regarded her firstborn thoughtfully.

The triplets with which she had begun her long family of nine, were twelve and a half now. Con, the present subject of their talk, still contrived to remain very much of a little girl; but a year spent in Canada had made Len grow up a good deal and being the eldest of the family had given her a sense of responsibility far beyond most English girls of her age. She looked up inquiringly.

"What is it, Mamma?"

"I want to talk seriously to you. I've got a job for you."

Len sat up, pushing the curly chestnut hair out of her eyes. "Con, do you mean? But I generally do. I can't do much about Margot as she's a whole form behind us and still counts as a Junior Middle. It makes it awkward. I wish she'd dig in properly and get up with us. She could do it if she liked. She's the really brainy one of us three."

"She's done much better this last year. I'm hoping she'll go on, now she's begun. But you know yourself, Len, that when you've gone on by spurts for at least six years you can't suddenly pull up and go ahead just as if you'd worked steadily all the time. Margot's still missing a lot of the grounding you two put in by working steadily from the first. And steady slogging isn't born in her, either."

"And when she's achieved it, I can hide my head in a bucket," Len said with a grin. "That's what makes me so mad. Margot could make rings round me if she chose."

"Well, you can leave Margot to herself. She's standing on her own feet now, and thank goodness for that! And so far as Con is concerned, it's high time she was doing the same. You people are well on the way to thirteen and she can't expect to have her eldest sister to run round after her all her school life. In fact, my lamb, it's ceasing this term—or I hope so. I've something else for you."

[1] The Chalet School Does it Again.

Len looked anxious. "I honestly don't think Con can help it. She's a bit like Nina Rutherford with her music, only it's writing in Con's case. You always say that music's the biggest part of Nina and writing's the biggest part of Con. What do you want me to do, anyhow?"

"I had a letter from Tom Gay this morning," Joey said, wisely giving up the question of Con for the moment.

"From Tom? Oh, how is she? Is she still as mad over Oxford as ever? When's she coming to see us all?"

"She didn't say. What she wrote about was something quite different—a new girl coming to the school."

"A pal of hers?" Len asked, looking alert.

"Not exactly. Give me my writing-case, will you, and you can read the letter."

Len jumped up to bring the writing-case and Joey fished out the letter in Tom Gay's curiously square handwriting. "I'm treating you as if you were grown-up over this, Len. It's between you and me, remember."

Len nodded. "Oh, of course. I won't talk. Am I to read it all?"

"No—from there." Joey pointed it out and Len curled up on the windowseat again and settled down to the reading. When she had finished she handed it back remarking, "I s'pose you want me to give a hand with this Rosamund girl."

"You've guessed it. That is exactly what I do want."

"It'll depend a lot on what form she's in," Len said.

"I can tell you that at once—Upper IVa, the same as yourself, so there won't be any difficulty about that."

"She's a year and a half older than me," Len ruminated.

"I know that; but you've one friend who is even more. It hasn't made too much difference there, has it? So it oughtn't to matter with Rosamund."

"No; but Prunella and I found each other, so to speak. Rosamund—I like her name, by the way—is being wished on to me and that's a cat of quite another colour."

"I don't want or expect you to have that sort of friendship with Rosamund unless you both want it after you've got to know each other. What I *do* want is you to look after her until she's found her feet. Put her into the way of doing things. You see, Len, you've been at boarding

17

school all your school life, more or less, but it'll all be quite new to her. You've seen what Tom says. She'll probably be all at sea at first—especially if she takes her ideas from silly schoolgirl weeklies," Joey said sapiently.

Len giggled. "She's in for a good many shocks if it's like that. They aren't much like the Chalet School! "

"You can't tell me anything about that. That's why I thought it a good idea if you'd hold her hand a little."

Len stood up. "I can't say anything straight away. I'll have to think it over. There's Con, you know——"

"I've told you I want Con to stand on her own feet now. Come, Len! Give me credit for never interfering with your friendships. I haven't asked you to take this girl to your bosom at once, but to help her out. You're the one in the family who sees things and is ready to help. I only want you to go a little way outside for the next few weeks. Once Rosamund has settled down, she'll probably find friends of her own and not need you so much."

But Len was a canny young person. "I daresay I'll do it, but I must have time to think it over. If I take it on, though, I'll *take* it on."

"That's all I ask," Joey said quietly. She was satisfied with this. Len had always been more cautious over beginning things than the others, but once she had made up her mind, she went on ungrudgingly.

"You won't tell the others, will you, Mamma?"

"Certainly not. I told you it was between you and me. Give me Cecil before you go. It's time for her feed and I promised I'd stay where I was today. Then you can rout Con out. If she's been mulling over a story all this time, she ought to get out and blow the cobwebs away. Tell her I said so. Oh, and tell Margot she can bring her work up here beside me in twenty minutes' time, will you?"

Len nodded. "O.K." She stooped over the cradle and lifted her baby sister. "She's a darling! And isn't she growing! Look! She's waking up! Hello, Precious! Her eyes are awfully dark, Mamma!"

"They'll turn black like mine I expect," Joey said, holding out her arms. "She's going to be just like me, everyone says, straight hair and all. Thank you, Len.

You're a most tremendous help to me these days. Oh, by the way, take Bruno with you when you go out."

"I don't know how you're going to manage when we're back at school," Len said, laying the baby in the outstretched arms. "You won't be able to go far with Cecil in a pram and Papa hasn't much time, and nor have Anna or the Coadjutor. It's a pity Beth left, isn't it?"

"Beth has far too much to do, getting ready for her wedding, to stay on here," her mother said, cuddling the baby.

Len giggled. "It's pricelessly funny! Beth's not so awfully old and she'll be aunt to Blossom Willoughby! Will Blossom call her 'Auntie', do you think?"

"Shouldn't imagine so. Now be off with you; and don't forget to give Margot my message."

"I never do forget messages," Len said with dignity as she picked up the cup and went out.

Left alone Joey gave her attention to her youngest who was beginning to give signs that she wanted her dinner. When the baby lay back against her arm, satisfied and sleepy, she settled herself comfortably in her chair and waited until the clatter of feet on the stairs told her that Margot, the youngest of the triplets, was coming.

"Had to wash her hands first I expect," Mrs. Maynard thought. "That unlucky garment of hers will need to be laundered before it goes to any poor orphan! Oh, well, I loathed sewing myself. I can't say much."

The door opened and she turned her head with a cheerful grin. "Come along, Misery, and take that look of tragedy off your face! You've got a long way on with that thing this last two days and if you stick at it today, you ought to finish it, all but the buttons and finishings-off and you'll still have tomorrow and Wednesday for fun."

"It's sickening having to sew like this in holidays," Margot grumbled as she came to sit down on the windowseat. She tossed down the rumpled thing that was growing into a nightdress intended for the poor child of an Innsbruck district which the school helped. During the war years, the help had ceased perforce, but since they had come back to the Oberland, Miss Annersley and Miss Wilson, co-Heads of the school, had got into touch with the parish priest and, for the past two years, the Christmas and Easter holidays had brought bundles of garments produced by the girls as holiday tasks.

Joey stretched out her hand. "Let me see how far you've got on. Margot, my pet, don't forget that this is for someone who mightn't have a nightie at all if it weren't for your work. Isn't that worth while?"

Margot shrugged. "Oh, I s'pose so. Yes, Mother, I really do know it but I do so loathe sewing. I've got the last sleeve to put in and there's all the tidying inside."

"I hope you've got the right sleeve into the right armhole," Joey said.

"Len reminded me about that before I began and helped me to fix it."

"Yes; that's what I'd expect of Len. You're lucky, Margot. Some sisters would have left you to muddle on."

Margot looked her surprise. "But she couldn't do *that*! We're triplets!" she said, stern rebuke in her voice.

Joey laughed. "How true! But triplets or not, you and Con rely far too much on Len. Now, Margot, I've finished casting-on. I'll race you. One line of knitting to an inch and a half of decent sewing. Are you ready? Go!"

This made a difference. Margot bent her red-gold head over her hated sewing and Joey set her needles flying and for a few minutes, there was silence. Then Joey cried, "Done!" and Margot held out her work for inspection.

"I *think* it's an inch and a half—from there to *there*."

Joey looked at it. "Oh, quite an inch and three-quarters, I think. And very decently sewn into the bargain. Dig in and you'll soon have the thing finished. Anna is packing for you three girls as I can't. Papa was murmuring last night about taking you five elder folk off for the day on Wednesday—to Berne. He has to go down, and he said something about taking you along. So get that garment done. You'd want to kick yourself if you played now and had to miss *that* fun."

"I jolly well should!" Margot snatched back her sewing and set to work with renewed vigour.

Joey chuckled to herself and picked up her knitting again and conversation languished for a short time In her cradle, Baby Cecil slumbered peacefully. The shouts of the boys came up from the side lawn where Stephen and Charles were instructing small Michael in the art of playing Tip and Run. Margot heard them and longed to be off to join them. She loved a good game of Tip and Run. Joey, keeping an eye on her, saw the restless look on her face and decided she had better administer another small verbal aid. The triplets were beginning to grow up quickly now.

"I must make the most of my time," she thought, rather panic-stricken. "They won't be hanging on my words of wisdom so trustfully much longer. Oh, dear! *Why* must children ever grow up? And yet in one way it's better. Len, at any rate, is a real companion, bless her. Con is young for her age, but Margot is even older in some ways than Len."

She finished her row and spread out the little forget-me-not blue frill that was the beginning of Felicity's skirt. Margot saw her and also looked admiringly at it.

"Is that for Felicity? She'll look a sweet in it," she said.

"Yes; she's small still, but even she does a certain amount of growing and she's certainly outgrown all last spring's frocks. I'll have to put them away till Cecil grows to them." She suddenly laughed. "And *when* Felicity's big enough, there are all those pretty summer frocks you three grew out of waiting for her."

"But won't they be out of date?" Margot asked as she rethreaded her needle.

"Not very likely. Children's clothes don't change much nowadays. Anyhow, out of date or not, we can't waste nine perfectly good ginghams. How's *your* work going?"

"I'm beginning to do the running. Then I've got to turn the edges and hem them and then, thank goodness, there's only the finishing off to do!" Margot heaved a sigh that nearly blew her work out of the window.

"And that's the most boring part of it all," Joey agreed. Then the golden voice that was one of her greatest gifts deepened. "Just the same, Mary Margaret Maynard, you be glad you can do it."

"Why?" Margot asked bluntly. "I don't see anything to be *glad* about it."

"Don't you? Have you forgotten that some day you'll

be meeting Our Lord and He can say to you then, 'Inasmuch as ye have done it for that poor child in Innsbruck ye did it for Me.' Isn't that rather worth while?"

"I hadn't thought of it that way," Margot said.

"But, my lamb, that's the best way *to* think of it. It isn't worth it if you only do it because you've got to—or have a row for not doing your holiday task. That's no use to you or anyone else. But if you remember that it's a little present for Him doesn't that make all the difference."

Margot bent her head over her sewing and Joey said no more. Instead, she turned the chatter to the question of tennis. But she noticed that this tempestuous daughter of hers sewed for her life for the rest of the time and when voices announced the return of the other two, the sleeve was practically finished.

"It's time you went to wash your hands," she said. "Leave that thing here and after lunch, you can come back and finish off. You'll have it all done by fifteen o'clock. Here; put it in my basket and scram! It's nearly thirteen and Anna will be sounding the gong."

Margot did as she was told, bent to kiss her mother and then to gaze adoringly at her baby sister. "Would it wake her if I gave her just the tiniest kiss?" she asked.

Joey grinned. "My motto is 'Let sleeping babes lie'," she said solemnly. "You can come up and help me wash her at bedtime and you can cuddle her then. I wouldn't, Margot. She's well away at the moment and if you *did* rouse her, she'd probably yell the house down."

"O.K., but it's awfully tantalising not to be able to kiss her when you like," Margot said reluctantly.

"You're going back to school soon and then you won't be tantalised any more," Joey said heartlessly. "You scram! And tell Con it's her turn to come up after dinner. You can come along and finish that grimy article of yours when she comes down. I must play fair."

"Oh, of course!" Margot went off and when she was fairly sure that they were all safely at their meal, Joey laid aside her knitting, took out the nightdress and looked at it.

"She might have been wiping the floor over with it! I'll just see to the neatenings for her. I think I might do so much. Then she can finish her sleeve and give it to

22

Anna to wash through. Mdlle. would have hysterics if she could see it as it is!" She went to work and by the time Jack Maynard and the tempting luncheon for both of them arrived, most of the neatening had been done.

"A good morning, I think," she told her husband as he sat down at the table between them and served her.

To herself she thought it had been a very good morning. She had got in some much needed help to Margot and she knew that Len would end by taking on the Gay scholarship winner. That would mean that her sisters must learn not to depend on her as much as they did.

"And that'll be a good thing!" she said to herself as she took her plate. "I won't have Len overburdened with responsibilities, even if she is the eldest."

CHAPTER III

A READY-MADE FRIEND

"Now have you got *everything*?" Joey, fully dressed, surveyed her triplet daughters as she put the question.

"Everything," Len said, swinging the small hand-case she carried. "And thank goodness Matey made us unpack yesterday along with Mary-Lou and the rest who live around here, so we don't have to worry about that."

"Very well. Off you go! I'll be seeing you shortly. Good-bye, my sugarpies! Be good girls and try your best this term." She swept them into her arms for a final hug and kissed them all round. "Scram! If I make you late, Auntie Hilda will have something to say to me!"

They laughed and turned. Then she called Len back. "Len! I've a note for Auntie Hilda. You other two go on and Len will catch you up. Shan't be a minute!"

"She'll have to be quick, then," Margot grinned as she turned once more to follow Con who had already set off. "Good-bye, Mother! Don't forget we're to come home on Sunday week! *You* remind her, Len. I must fly!"

She set off, red gold curls tossing, long legs covering the ground rapidly.

Joey arrived a minute later with the note. "Here you

are! Thank goodness I remembered in time. Tell Auntie Hilda she can ring me after Mittagessen."

Len took the note and held up her face for a last kiss. "Margot told me to remind you about Sunday week. You won't forget, will you? It'll be ten days since we've seen Cecil and it's quite long enough. She's growing so!"

"It's a habit tiny babies have," Joey said solemnly. "No; I won't forget. Anyhow, we shall probably meet during walks. You can always *look* at her, you know."

"That's not the same thing as cuddling her. You won't let us take her out of the pram, 'specially if she's asleep."

"You're quite right; I won't. 'Let sleeping babes lie' is one of my firmest maxims as I've told you often."

"I know. But you *will* try to fix your walks with the kids when we have ours so that we do meet kind of accidental done-a-purpose, won't you?"

"Where on earth did you pick up *that* expression?" Joey demanded.

"Heard you use it to Papa last week," Len told her.

"You would! It's plain to be seen that you've inherited my fly-paper memory if nothing else! All right; I'll do what in me lies. But don't blame me if whoever is in charge refuses to let you stop."

"They won't," Len said shrewdly. "They'll all be dying to have a peep at Cecil. It's only the people who've been up in the hols that have seen her and the rest were all raging when they had to go off at the end of last term without the tiniest squint at her."

Joey chuckled. "I can well imagine. We timed things rather well, she and I. It's time you were off. Con and Margot will have reached school by this time."

"And the coaches ought to be up in about ten minutes' time," Len agreed with a glance at the watch which had marked her twelfth birthday. "O.K. Good-bye, Mamma. Don't try to do too much when we're not here to help you."

"Not nearly so much to do now you and the boys have gone. And Papa rang me up very early this morning to say that he thinks he's found someone to take Beth's place, so I'll be on velvet after she arrives. Good-bye, my biggest big girl! Enjoy yourself and look after Rosamund and don't worry about me!" She tugged the shining curly tail which Len wore tied back from her face and then turned resolutely and went back into the house while Len made off across the lawn, shouting over her shoulder, "Mind you let us know all about her as soon as you can!"

Joey laughed, waved her hand and went in to tackle her four youngest. Until halfway through the Easter holidays just ended, she had had an old friend's daughter as Mother's Help and nursery governess; but now Beth Chester had gone home to prepare for a June wedding and so far they had had no one to take her place.

"Still," Mrs. Maynard thought as she climbed the stairs to the playroom, "I'm lucky with Anna and the Coadjutor. Some poor folk have to manage without any help whatsoever!" A sudden squall from her youngest son made her quicken her steps and she burst into the playroom in time to stop a stand-up fight between him and Michael.

Meanwhile, Len darted across the garden, through the gate and round the main building of the Chalet School to the girls' entrance. She made for the Splashery appropriated to the members of both Upper Fourths and changed her shoes before joining her sisters and the little group of girls of all ages who had come up early.

They were gathered in the wide entrance hall, waiting for the arrival of the main body of the school and one or two called to her when she appeared.

"Can't stop! I've got a note for the Head!" Len hissed at them as she shot across the hall and disappeared down a corridor leading to a wing of the building where the study, the office and the stockroom had all been removed during the Christmas holidays.

A long-legged individual of nearly sixteen, whose shapely head was covered with a short fuzz of golden-brown curls, grinned placidly at the rest. "Zeal, all zeal!" she remarked. "So Len's tying her mop back. You've got pigtails, Con, I see. What's Margot doing—oh, bobbed as usual."

"I'm not looking for extra work," Margot said with a toss of her short mop.

"Aunt Joey never has dressed you all alike, has she?"

"Mother says we aren't really alike so there's no point in it," Margot replied. "Anyhow, look at you with curls instead of Kenwigses! And after all this time, too! I never remember you with short hair before."

"I did, though. I had a straight bob when I was a small kid and then Gran insisted that it was time I started to grow it; so I did. But you're right, Margot. I had pigtails all the time you knew me until last term."

"That's what comes of being in a messy accident," said a tiny, silvery-voiced girl who stood close by. "Mary-Lou, you can't complain, seeing you've got curls out of it."

Mary-Lou grinned down affectionately at her. "And an enormous saving in time in the mornings! But I *was* mad with Uncle Jack when I first found out what he'd done," she added reflectively. "I could have gnawed chunks out of him!"

A sturdy person of fifteen chuckled. "Godmother would have had a lot to say to you if you *had*!"

"There was that, too, of course," Mary-Lou assented. "Keep your wool on, young Jo. I *didn't* do it—listen!" She suddenly interrupted herself. "Isn't that a horn? Yes; there they come—you can just see them round the corner through the trees. Scoot, Con, and tell the Heads they're here."

Before Con could obey her, Len came flying back like a rocket and the next moment two tall women followed her—the co-Heads of the Chalet School. The girls moved back from the door, and the one whose curly white mop showed streaks of copper, smiled at them.

"Don't go too far away. You'll be needed to help with cases, I expect," she said, laughing, before she went on to stand beside her colleague in the great doorway.

The first coach rolled up and came to a stop. Another minute, and the girls began to pour out.

Miss Annersley, the leader of the two Heads, instantly called, "Lines down the drive, girls! And keep to forms!"

As the now empty coaches moved away, the girls sorted themselves and by the time the last had gone, the drive was lined with girls of every age, including Rosamund, who took her place shyly between the two girls who had looked after her during the long journey.

Rosamund Lilley had been living in a whirl ever since that Friday afternoon when Miss Keatinge had kept her behind and told her what was going to happen. She was no more reconciled to her fate now than she had been then; but so far she had managed to keep her feelings to herself. Now, as she stood between Alicia Leonard and Betty Landon, she felt shyer and more unhappy than ever.

"But I've got to stick it somehow," she told herself as Alicia gently pulled her round into the line that was forming across the drive. "Mrs. Gay put it up to me that this is their thank-offering. Oh, if only I knew *some*one! It's being so all alone with strangers that's so awful!"

A few minutes later, her wish was to be gratified. Miss Annersley welcomed the school in the musical voice which was one of her greatest assets, Joey Maynard always declared, and then told the girls to come in and not to make so much noise that the people at the Sanatorium at the other end of the Platz would hear, and then left them to it, for she and Miss Wilson, her co-Head, had more work than they quite knew how to manage, anyhow.

A slight, puckish-faced girl who, Alicia had informed Rosamund, was the Head Girl, took charge. "School—turn!" she ordered. "March to your Splasheries and change for Kaffee und Kuchen and be quick about it."

"Do we go to common rooms when we're ready, Betsy?" asked a charmingly pretty person of Betsy's age. "Or may we go out into the garden?"

"Common rooms! The bell will ring in ten minutes," Betsy replied. "Anyhow, you're in charge of Upper III, Blossom, so you won't have time."

Blossom—Rosamund thought her name suited her appearance—nodded. "I'd forgotten that. Come along, Upper Thirds! Follow me to the school Splasheries. Janice and Judy, stop sparring! I know it's first day, but that's no excuse for a free-for-all in the entrance hall!"

The two ten-year-olds who had been surreptitiously scrapping over a suitcase, stopped on the word and Blossom marched off with her band of leggy Juniors. Then a prefect, chiefly distinguished by heavy brown plaits swung round her shapely head and very blue eyes, came to where the girls with whom Rosamund had travelled were standing and told them to come to her and be quick about it.

They were marched across the hall, down a narrow

passage and into a light airy room with toilet basins against one wall and light stands with pegs set across from side to side. Most of the girls went straight to claim their own pegs. Rosamund stood on one side, wondering what she ought to do. Then some of her troubles ended for a slim, leggy girl who seemed to be her own age and whose chestnut locks were tied back from her face to dangle in a curly tail down her back, came up to her.

"I know you're Rosamund Lilley," she said, speaking in a very clear voice. "I'm Len Maynard and I'm in charge of you for the present. Come along. I've found your peg and locker. You're next to me." She led the way and pointed out an empty peg on which she directed Rosamund to hang her coat and beret before taking her to the shoe-lockers, which lined the farther end of the room, and opened one of the little doors. "Here you are! This is your locker. Got your house shoes in your case? Oh, good! One up to you! Lots of people forget and send them in their trunks and that means a word or two from Matey—Matron, I mean. She's death on that sort of thing. Change your shoes and put your outdoors in here."

A mop-headed creature with wicked blue eyes came up at this moment. "Hallo, Len! How's your mother? And when are we to see the new baby?"

"Oh, hello, Heather!" Len said. "They're both fine and Mamma's promised that she'll arrange to take Cecil for her walks when we have ours so that we can meet. She's a perfect pet—Cecil, I mean." She turned to Rosamund. "She's my new baby sister and as she was born at the very end of last term, everyone's dying to see her. Changed? Then come and wash and tidy your hair. Shove up, Maeve, and let Rosamund have a chance."

Maeve chuckled and moved about two inches to the side of the basin where another girl was also washing her hands. " 'Fraid that's the best I can do." She gave Rosamund a friendly grin. "It's always a scrum in here. Oh, Len, Mummy sent her love to you all and she and Daddy are hoping to come out in June and then you'll all see *my* baby sister. You aren't the only one, you know!"

"I know that; but Daphne's an old story now!" Len retorted. "Who's she like?"

"The living image of Auntie Madge—Mummy says just like Rix was at her age. Who's Cecil like?"

"Daddy says only herself; but the rest of us think she's a lot like Con."

"Only 'cos she's so dark," Con herself observed, leaving an excited group of girls with whom she had been exchanging news. "*I* think she's going to be exactly like Mamma."

"*Will* you folk stop nattering and finish changing and get off to your common room?" Katharine interposed at that point. "I'm going to give you two more minutes and then I'm clearing the Splash whether you're done or not."

Squeals of dismay greeted this and all chatter ceased while the girls scrambled to finish off. Len chuckled and slipped a chummy hand through Rosamund's arm. "You're ready now, aren't you? So are we. Let's clear. It'll leave more room for the rest. Come on, Con! Oh, and this is Rosamund Lilley, by the way—Tom Gay's friend."

Con smiled at the new girl. "What a lovely name you have!" she said dreamily.

Len looked sharply at her. "Con!" she said warningly. "Don't forget what you promised Mamma."

Con's creamy cheeks went pink. "Oh, I won't! I promise you I won't! But it *is* a lovely name, all the same."

Rosamund, who had been well jeered at by Joan Baker for her name, crimsoned. "Are you making game of me?" she asked bluntly.

"Of course not!" Con sounded shocked. "It really is a most lovely name. You won't mind if I use it in one of my stories some time, will you, Rosamund?"

"Con writes stories and poems," Len explained. "She wants to be like Mamma and write books some day."

"Does your Mum write stories?" Rosamund exclaimed.

"Yes. I expect you know them," Con said earnestly. "Have you read *Cecily Holds the Fort*—or *Werner of the Alps*—or *A Royalist Soldier-Maid*? That was her last one, all about the Civil War."

Rosamund was standing stockstill. "But that's Josephine M. Bettany!" she exclaimed. "Of course I've read her books. I got them from the school library and the Free Library. My eldest sister and her husband gave me *A Royalist Soldier-Maid* for Christmas."

"That's Mamma," Len said with would-be nonchalance. "She was Miss Bettany before she married Papa and she still writes under her old name."

"Well, talk of lucky!" Rosamund had been startled out of her bashfulness. "I think you two are *jolly* lucky to have *her* for your Mum!"

"We don't call her that," Con said. "She doesn't like it. We call her Mamma—or Mother. Margot always does, but Len and I forget and anyhow I *like* 'Mamma'."

"You see," Len explained swiftly, "when we were in Canada, she was afraid we might start saying 'Mom' and 'Pop', so she was awfully strict about it. We could call them 'Mamma and Papa', or 'Father and Mother', or we might say 'Daddy', but she forbade anything else."

"Oh," Rosamund said blankly. "I didn't know."

"Of course you didn't. And here's the common room. Come on in and see it."

Rosamund went with them into a big, sunny room with flowering plants, a large cage of canaries which were singing deafeningly, and a variety of chairs of all kinds from comfortable wicker easy-chairs full of cushions to gay little peasant stools, painted with clusters of flowers and fruit. A big table, loaded with magazines was at one side and there were two or three smaller ones in the windows between the cretonne curtains. A great white tiled stove stood in one corner and round three of the walls ran shelves of books, most of which looked well-read.

"This is where we Middles spend our free time when we aren't out," Len said, pushing over a chair. "All the houses have their own common rooms. The Juniors have a smaller room, there are fewer of them and they haven't so many books; but they have lots of games. The Seniors are at the other end of the corridor and theirs is more—more drawing-roomy. How do you like ours?"

Rosamund looked round the pretty room. "Oh, awfully. What piles of books! Can we have a lend of them when we like?"

The Maynards looked at each other. On the whole, they were inclined to like Rosamund, but she did say some awfully queer things, and while they wanted to keep her out of trouble with the prefects and mistresses, they hardly liked to correct her English. Len gave it up. It was beyond her.

"You can borrow whenever you like from here," she said. "They are our own books. Middles have given them all through the time the school's been a school. The only rule is that we take care of them and put them back in the proper place. Are you fond of reading, Rosamund?"

Rosamund, who had been frequently accused of "forever having her nose in a book," looked at the richness before her and said simply, "Well, rather!"

"Oh, good! So're we," Con said. "Margot, our other sister—we're triplets, you know—doesn't care about it nearly as much as we do."

Rosamund stared. "I thought you said your new sister was called Cecil?" she said. "Oh, but you said triplets!"

Len nodded. "Margot's our third. She isn't in the same House, though. She's in St. Agnes. But we have Felicity as well. She and Felix are twins. There's nine of us altogether now."

Rosamund looked startled again. She was one of six and had always understood that they were a large family. Nine children struck her as being out of the common run. "*Nine*, did you say?" she asked.

Len laughed and nodded. "Yes; isn't it fun? Mamma says she always meant to beat all the others—our aunts and uncles, you know—and when Auntie Mollie had Daphne last October she simply had to have another to keep well ahead. That made seven for them. You've seen our cousin Maeve, haven't you? She's one of them. Bride's at St. Mildred's—the house further along the road—and Peggy was there until last summer. She's grown-up, of course. She's nineteen now. And then there are the three boys, Rix, John and Maurice."

"And Auntie Madge has six," Con chimed in. "Sybil is a prefect here, *and* in the Sixth, and Josette is in Upper V and Ailie in IIa. They have three boys, too."

"Now that's enough about us," Len said. "There's heaps of time to tell her any more she wants to know. Tell us about you, Rosamund. Have you any brothers and sisters besides the married one?"

The bell rang just then and Rosamund was startled to

note that the chatter which had become almost deafening, died away at once with a stunning suddenness. Everyone stopped talking and made for the door to form into line. They went in a particular order, for two or three people squeezed in between others. Con jumped up and ran to a big notice board at the end of the room, coming back to announce, "O.K. She's sitting between you and Maeve, Len. And she's in your dormy, too."

"Who's that talking?" demanded Katharine.

"I was only telling the new girl where she sits," Con said.

Katharine smiled at Rosamund. "I see. That's all right. Len, you're in charge for the moment, aren't you?"

Len nodded. "Yes. And please, Katharine, she's in my dormy, too, so may I take her up after Kaffee und Kuchen and show her?"

"By all means," Katharine said. "Go to your places now. *Now* are you all ready? Forward, then, Heather! "

Heather—the mop-head—led the way into the corridor down which a long file of older girls was marching in silence. The rest tailed on behind and after them came a crowd of girls Rosamund had noticed in their common room.

She found that the dining-room was just as attractive with tables set round the walls and across the room with cloths of coloured checks, gay china and baskets of fancy bread-twists. There were plates of ivory butter and dishes of jam. Also plates of odd-looking white oblongs which were sugar. And she had another shock when someone asked her if she would have coffee or milk.

Maeve Bettany, who sat at her left hand, explained. "We don't have tea here. Which would you like?"

Rosamund collected her wits and chose coffee and presently everyone was served and they were all sitting eating the delicious twists with butter and jam while the buzz of talk went on quietly. Once, when it rose beyond bounds, Betsy Lucy at another table with a number of other girls who all looked either grown-up or very nearly so, got up, went to the top table which was vacant, and rang a bell and the noise died down.

Len and Con had little chance of more talk with the

new girl just then. Everyone wanted to know about Baby Cecil. Then the others had news of their own to tell. Rosamund ate her meal quickly, replying when she was spoken to, but venturing no remarks on her own. She noticed that though no mistress was present, the girls' manners were as good as those Mum insisted on at home. No one snatched or reached out for things and everyone took care that no one was neglected.

Towards the end of the meal, Len took the opportunity when the others were discussing tennis to turn to the new girl and ask, "Can you speak French or German?"

"No," Rosamund said shyly. "I've never learnt any."

"Oh, well, you'll soon pick it up here. You see, we have two days each week when we speak nothing but French and two days when it's nothing but German."

"What—lessons, too?" Rosamund gasped.

"Oh, yes. Lessons and walks and games and everything. But it isn't so bad, you know. Hearing it all round you, you can't help learning it. And then everyone's ready to help you." She paused to turn and survey Rosamund thoughtfully. "*You'll* be all right! You don't look a dud at all and even duds like Heather can manage *some*."

"What's that about me?" demanded Heather from the other end of the table.

"I was only saying you were a dud at languages."

"How right you are!" Heather bit into a large slice of cake and munched it before grinning at Rosamund chummily and asking, "Are you a dud at 'em, too?"

"I—I've never learned any," Rosamund faltered.

Heather grinned again. "Welcome, fellow dud! Though I expect you'll soon beat me into fits," she added with a gusty sigh. "You look as if you might be a Nib."

"Rubbish!" said a girl older than the others. "You could do well enough if you really tried, Heather."

"That's all you know," Heather said darkly.

However, at that point, Betsy sounded the bell for the end of the meal and they had to clear the table before they left the room.

Len and Con escorted Rosamund to the door of the Marigold dormitory where Con left the other two and

33

went off on her own concerns while Len ushered the new girl into the room and showed her her cubicle.

Rosamund's ideas of boarding-school life had been mainly culled from *The Schoolgirl's Pal* and *The Schoolgirl's Paragon* and she was greatly impressed to find that instead of having a bed in a roomful of others, here she had her own little cubicle. She admired the dainty place with its white walls, curtains of reversible cretonne patterned with quaintly formal nosegays of marigolds and rug to match at the side of her bed which had a coverlet of deep orange. Len explained that this had to be removed and folded every night before she introduced the novice to her bureau with its locker at one end, two small drawers and two long ones running the whole length of the article. The mirror was in the lid of the locker on the underside and, as Len explained, you might set out your photos, books and any ornaments you had over the other part.

"Only you have to hand in the books first to be passed," she added. "Oh, you haven't brought any. Never mind, we've plenty belonging to the school and most of the rest of us are willing to lend. We'll unpack your nightcase and that's all you can do tonight. Tomorrow you'll unpack your trunk. Come into my cubey and I'll show you how Matey likes things done. We three are unpacked because we live up here and came in yesterday morning to get it out of the way."

She held up one of the curtains which separated the cubicles and Rosamund found herself in the twin of her own except that this one had a lived-in look, for Len had framed snapshots standing on her bureau and a collection of miniature models of animals as well as half-a-dozen story books standing against the wall between a pair of book-ends.

"My cousin Bride Bettany sent me those for Christmas," she said, nodding at them. "They're rather sweet, aren't they. Mine are cocker spaniels and she sent Con a pair of cats and Margot rabbits. She carved them herself. She's taken up woodcarving and she gave everyone something."

"Are these all your brothers and sisters?" Rosamund asked, looking at the snaps.

"Yes. That one's the three boys—Steve, Charles and

Mike. Here are us three and this is Mamma and the twins. Here's Papa. And this is Mamma's new St. Bernard, Bruno. He's a sweet, but awfully wicked. This," Len picked it up with a loving look, "is our darling old Rufus. He died three years ago of old age, Papa said. He was just seventeen and Mamma got him when she was only thirteen. It was dreadful losing him, but he wasn't ill, thank goodness. We came down one morning and found him lying dead in the drawing-room on the bearskin rug where he slept. We missed him horribly, but it was just before we went to Canada or it would have been worse. I never remember a time till he died when Rufus wasn't there." She set the snap down and then said they had better go downstairs and she would show Rosamund the Hall.

On the whole, she contrived to keep the new girl so busy that there was no time for thinking of home. She performed her final good deed by deliberately breaking rules and slipping through the cubicle curtains just after Lights Out to say good-night to a Rosamund wondering if she was going to cry herself to sleep or not.

"Visiting isn't allowed," she whispered, "but I thought I might just come to say good-night. Good-night, Rosamund. Sleep well! See you in the morning! "

She administered a pat to the shoulder nearest her and was gone. Rosamund, her heart warm with the kindness of the thought, decided to put off her weeps for another night and fell asleep before another five minutes was up.

CHAPTER IV

EARLY DAYS

"DEAR EVERYONE, This is a letter for you all because we have so little time for writing letters. We do them on Saturday mornings when we have finished prep and mending, and we can write on Sundays between breakfast (which you call Froostick here, though that isn't the right way to spell it) and church. I'm sending this to you, Mum and Dad, and please pass it on to the rest when you've read it so that everyone gets my news.

"Well, Mum, it isn't bad here, though funny after St. Matthew's. One thing is you don't call the teachers teachers. They're mistresses or masters. Mostly, we have mistresses, but art and singing and things like that are taught by masters and some of the girls have masters for things like chello and fiddle. We have one girl who is marvelous and she has someone very special called Hair Airnst fon Aberhard. At least that's the way she says it but it's spelt different. Her name is Nina Rutherford and she has no father or mother but only cousins.

"I have made a friend already. Her name is Len Maynard and she is one of triplets. The other two are Con and Margo. And oh, Mum, their mother is Josephine M. Bettany that wrote that smashing book our Dorothy and Peter gave me for Christmas. Len says they have all she ever wrote in the library here and I'm going to read them. She is a friend of Miss Gay's that wrote to her about me coming and Len said she asked her to give me a helping hand at first. Only now we are really chums. She is a year and seven months younger than I am but she is very clever and in the same form. They all learnt to talk French and German from being babies and she and Con are helping me a lot. Margo is in another form. But I can say please and thank you and yes and no and things like that in French and German already and please tell Mrs. Gay I mean to try hard and get on.

"I think I'm going to like it here after all. I told Len *I* had a scholarship and she said, 'Good for you!' and thumped me on the back. We have form gardens, Dad, and our form has one of the big borders down the drive. We were gardening last night and Katharine Gordon who's our special prefect said I seemed to know a lot and I said, 'You see, Dad's a market gardener and I've always helped him.' Then one of the big girls who was standing near said so was her dad and when she was through Coll she was going in with him and we must have a chat about it."

Rosamund blotted her sixth sheet, laid it aside and began on the next. She had only numbered it, however, when the bell rang for the end of Saturday morning work and she had to scrabble the pages together. She heaved a deep sigh. There was such a lot to write about here!

36

"What's the why of that?" Len Maynard demanded as they went down the corridor to the Speisesaal.

Rosamund stared at her. "What d'you mean?"

"I only asked why you were sighing like a mad storm wind. You nearly blew me out of the form room and into the Speisesaal!" Len giggled.

Rosamund giggled, too. "What awful rot! We weren't anywhere near it, anyhow!"

"I know that. But you were just like an eighty-miles-an-hour gust of wind! What's wrong? Lemonade or milk?"

"Lemonade, please. I didn't mean it. Only I've got such a lot to write about and I haven't got a tenth of it down yet."

"Jiminy cricket! You *must* have piles to say. You've been going it as hard as you could for the last half-hour. Here's your glass. Come and grab your biscuits—ooh! It's buns; not biscuits! Karen really is a complete poppet!" Len helped herself to a bun, saw that Rosamund took hers, and then they moved away to a window where there were seven or eight others, sipping at their glasses and chattering as hard as they could go in between whiles.

"You see," Rosamund explained, "I want to tell them everything and we have so little time for writing letters."

"You'll have between Frühstück and Church tomorrow morning—and the early afternoon, too, if you haven't finished then. That ought to be enough, surely."

"But there's such lots to tell about," Rosamund sighed.

"Oh, well, you must do what you can and go on with it next Saturday. It'll be a kind of serial—sort of 'To be continued in our next'!" Len giggled at her own wit. "Finished? Then come on out into the garden."

"I'll tell you what would be even better," put in Betty Landon who had been listening to all this. "Make a diary of it and do a bit every night after Abendessen when we're free. Ask Deney if you can buy an exercise-book from Stationery and when it's full, send it home and get another and go on with that. I should think your folk would be thrilled!"

Rosamund prepared to consider this idea, but Len was before her. "What a super idea, Betty! That's just the very thing! You do that, Rosamund. Finish up this letter and tell your folk what you're going to do. On Monday we'll ask Miss Dene for the book—and you can easily put in twenty minutes or so each evening and then your people will know all about what you're doing. In fact, I've a good mind to do it myself," she went on meditatively. "It would be fun to have a diary to read when I'm old and remember the fun we used to have."

"Wouldn't it?" Betty was impressed by her own idea. "I think I'll have a go myself."

And that was the beginning of a craze which kept Upper IVa, at any rate, well out of mischief for most of that term. The others took to it like ducks to water when they heard about it and Miss Dene had a pile of requests for exercise-books to deal with on the Monday when the Stationery prefect, Leila Norris, brought the list for her signature at the end of the morning. She inquired into the matter, gave her approval and told Leila to issue the books.

Thus advised, Rosamund prepared for the walk happily and next day did as Len had advised her—wrote all she could in the time allowed and wound up by saying that she meant to keep a diary which she would send in due course.

Her home letters came all in one envelope and she scurried off to find a quiet corner to enjoy them. She had fits of homesickness, despite the fact that conditions at the Chalet School were much better than she had expected. She found her corner, curled up and spread the five letters out, and picked up her mother's first.

Mrs. Lilley had not the pen of a ready writer, but something in the two sheets she had filled brought back the atmosphere of home and nearly reduced Rosamund to tears.

"It was nice to get your long letter. It came by the midday post, so I got a good read at it while I had my dinner. When the rest came home for tea I read it out to them and then gave it to our Dorothy when she came in next day to show me some knitting she has been doing.

"I am glad you have made a nice friend. I never liked Joan Baker for you and Dad did not either. But she will not matter to us any more. Mr. Baker has had a big win on the Pools and Mrs. Baker told me this morning that they are leaving here and going to live in Worthing. Joan is still there but Mrs. B. says she must come home till they remove. They are selling most of their things and buying all new. Mr. Baker has been talking to Dad over the garden wall and he has just come in and told me Mr. B. means to buy a car and they will send Joan and Pam to a good school. Dad says he can see it will be easy come easy go with them unless Mrs. Baker's father or someone can make them see sense. Dad is going to mention it to Canon Gay if he gets a chance. And you remember that it is silly to spend all you have got for then where are you?

"Edna Baker has left her job and she's sent Reg Harrison his ring back. Kath Stevens came on an errand for her mother and asked about you. You might write to her, Rosamund, if your teachers let you. Kath says Joan has written to say that she hopes she will understand but now she is going to a grand school she can't go on being friends with girls who only go to the Parish. Kath was real hurt about it. I should not like to think you would ever be like that, Rosamund. You remember that when it comes to the end we are all just flesh and blood however grand and wonderful we may have been. Besides such behaviour is unkind and rude as well and bad manners are something I never would allow and I will not now.

"The budgie missed you but is beginning to talk again. Dad whistled and talked to him and he is happier.

"I must finish now as my bread is ready to work up. Be a good girl and try to please your teachers and remember your manners. My Miss Rosamund that you are called after used to say anyone could be a lady if she thought and acted in a ladylike manner and that is what I have tried to teach you, all of you.

Good-bye for now and lots of love,
Your loving Mother.

"P.S. We shall put all our letters into one envelope. Dorothy has some grand news but she is writing herself."

Rosamund read it twice before she kissed it and tucked it into the breast-pocket of her blazer. Dad's was a brief note. Letter-writing was even less in his line than in his wife's, beyond telling Rosamund that they were all proud of her and he hoped she would keep them so by being a good girl and a good scholar, he had not much to say. Dorothy's letter was very brief, written in curly, decorative handwriting that filled up the pages quickly.

"I've left the best news to the very end," she wound up. "How will you like being an Aunt? It won't be till October some time, but you can be knitting some little socks if you like, or a matinée coat and cap. Make them blue and I'll send you the money for the wool."

Rosamund flushed and her eyes sparkled. "Dorothy's going to have a baby! How lovely! I must tell Len. She could ask her mother to lend me a pattern for the coat and cap. And I must write to her by herself. I'm glad Betty thought of keeping a diary because I won't have much time for letters to everyone at the week-end."

She turned to her brothers' brief notes and finished up with the lengthy screed contributed by her high school sister, Charmian. Charmian had been luckier than Rosamund in that matter and had entered the High School with flying colours. She would be eighteen at the end of the term and had already been accepted as a probationer at the children's hospital. She was a little patronising, for she felt that no private school could hope to come up to "The High" in the matter of lessons, at any rate. She advised Rosamund to work hard at her languages.

"You're getting a marvellous chance there," she wrote. "If you do really well, you might get one of the County Schols to Baddeley College and be there while I'm at the hospital and get your letters then be a teacher at the High or somewhere like that. You'd get good money and smashing hols as well. It would be worth any amount of hard work for that. I might have thought of it myself, but I've always wanted to be a nurse. It's up to you. What about it?"

Charmian had her own ideas, too, about Mr. Baker's astounding good luck. "I shouldn't have minded if it had been Dad won that £25,000. But if it had been him, I hope we shouldn't have been putting on all the airs Edna is. And I should *still* have wanted to be a nurse. I don't see Mum going off her head over it like Mrs. Baker."

"I'm sure she wouldn't," Rosamund thought as she

added Charmian's letter to the others in her pocket, and
went off to find Len and tell her all about Dorothy and ask
if she thought Mrs. Maynard would lend her a pattern for
the little coat.

Len, questioned, not only agreed that they had *piles* of
patterns for baby woollies but offered to ask her mother to
show Rosamund how to set to work on it.

"We're going home on Sunday in the afternoon," she
said. "I'll ask if you can come with us. Go to Mdlle and
ask her about the wool. She keeps hundreds of bundles of
all colours and kinds and needles as well. She'll fit you out
and we can take it with us on Sunday and Mamma will
start you off. Oh, lovely being an Aunt at your age!"

"Mamma was an aunt when *she* was only fourteen or
fifteen," put in Con who was standing by listening. "That's
all she was when Peggy and Rix Bettany were born."

Rosamund went pink. "I—I didn't mean to ask for an
invite," she faltered.

The pair stared at her. "But you didn't!" Len cried. "It
was me suggested it. Anyhow, Mamma nearly always has
the new girls to tea their first term, so that'll be all right.
You go and talk it over with Mdlle, Rosamund."

Con, who had been watching the new girl dreamily,
spoke up. "She's scared of Mdlle. Let's go with her and
help her out, Len. You know," delicately, "how Mdlle is
about French and Rosamund hasn't done much so far."

As this was largely what was at the bottom of Rosamund's demurring expression, she relaxed with relief. "I
know so awfully little," she said.

"I know; and we ought all to be talking it this minute,"
Len reminded them. "Come on, Rosamund. I'll tell you
how to say that in French and you repeat it. You'll soon
learn. *You* aren't one of the duds!"

Rosamund went pink at this compliment and did her
best with the French Len coaxed her to repeat at least a
dozen times. When at last the young woman nodded, she
felt that that particular remark was graven into her
memory for all time, even if she couldn't say it with the
pretty accent of the triplets. However, both Len and Con
assured her it would come in time. Then the bell rang and
they had to go in for German Dictat, during which time,

Rosamund was set to learning a list of German phrases with Miss Denny, who took them, coming every now and then to help her with pronunciation, and Dorothy's wonderful news slipped to the back of her mind.

CHAPTER V

A NEW DEVELOPMENT

MISS ANNERSLEY sat in the study, reading and re-reading a letter which had come for her two days earlier. She looked up at her co-Head who was checking up on some book lists. "Nell!"

"Um?" Miss Wilson murmured, giving half an ear.

Miss Annersley looked at her and realised it. She rose from her seat, crossed to the table where Miss Wilson was working and, without apology or ceremony, plucked the lists away and tossed them into a nearby armchair.

Miss Wilson sat up and gave her a startled look. "And what, may I ask, is the meaning of that?" she demanded.

"I want your whole attention—and considered advice. Leave those wretched book lists alone for a few minutes and lend me all your ears!"

"You talk as if I had at least fifty," Miss Wilson said indignantly. "Well, you've deprived me of my proper job, so you may as well hold forth. Where's my cigarette case? Have one? Oh, then I *will*. Now go ahead and be brief."

"You talk as if I were in the habit of burbling hopelessly!" It was Miss Annersley's turn to sound indignant.

"I don't; but Rosalie wants those book lists checked so that she can order and I said she should have them this afternoon. However, now I look at you I see you have a somewhat wild and woolly look about you. Granted that you are no longer young, you're still as fair as ever you were——"

She stopped short perforce, for Miss Annersley had set a firm hand across her lips. "That's enough rubbish for one time. Read this and give me your considered opinion." And she thrust her letter into her colleague's hands.

Nell Wilson glanced at her and gave up her teasing

promptly. It was clear that her friend was in sober earnest. She gave her attention to the sheets given to her.

"Dear Madam, I write to enquire if you have a vacancy in your school for my elder grand-daughter. She is fourteen and will be fifteen at the end of November.

"Circumstances have altered considerably in my family of late and it is necessary that both the girls should now receive a better education than they have done hitherto. My elder grand-daughter wishes to be entered for your school. She already knows one of your pupils, recently become a member thereof and has heard of the Chalet School as being one where foreign languages are taught. As she is anxious to perfect herself in these, she feels that to live in a foreign country would be one of the best means of attaining her wish. The younger girl will attend a very good school at Hastings for the present. If her sister should do well and be happy at your establishment, she will be entered with you in due course.

"Naturally, it is desirable that she should lose as little time as possible so I write to ask if it would be convenient to you to accept her at once. I enclose a Bank reference together with stamped addressed envelope for the early reply with which I trust you will oblige, my dear Madam.

"Yours faithfully,
"HERBERT WILLIAM BAKER."

Miss Wilson read this screed twice through. Then she laid it down. "Who on earth is he?"

"You know as much as I do. The address is Worthing. I don't think we have a single Worthing girl here."

"We haven't," Miss Wilson asserted. "However, that's nothing to go by. He doesn't give us the girl's name. Baker, I suppose. Well, what are you going to do?"

"I don't know. For one thing, he doesn't say anything about her earlier education and I like to know something about that. For another, the term is a fortnight old and, as you know, I don't like taking people unless they come at the beginning of term. What do you think, Nell? Should I send him a prospectus and say we can't take her this term, but shall have one or two vacancies next?"

"It would be one way out. On the other hand, what

will they do with the girl? Send her back to her old school? I hope they won't let her kick her heels at home until September. Fourteen's a bad age for that sort of thing."

"Almost the worst age possible." Miss Annersley picked up the letter and considered it again. "You see he says that she knows one of our new girls. That would probably mean Rosamund Lilley and she's been problem enough, goodness knows, considering she came to us not knowing a word of French or German."

"But doesn't she come from Meadowfield? That isn't anywhere near Worthing, is it? He says 'recently', so that may mean back to September. You can't go round asking all the girls who have come to us between then and now if they know a girl from Worthing named Something Baker. We don't even know if he's her paternal or maternal grandparent. The name may be something different."

"I know that. That's what helps to make it so difficult. I'd write to Madge Russell, but she's up to the eyes at present and anyhow, Worthing is a long way from Llan-y-penllan and the chances are she couldn't do anything about it." Miss Annersley frowned as she skimmed through the pages once more. "I think this is where we consult the others. What's the time?"

"Coffee time," Miss Wilson said with a glance at her watch. She tossed the end of her cigarette out of the open window and stood up. "That's an idea, Hilda! Come on! Let's take two cups up and tell them we've come to coffee with them. It certainly is a puzzle and they may as well exercise their brains on it. Some of them will have to deal with this girl if we decide to have her."

She went to a cupboard and fished out two cups and saucers. "Is this biscuits? Chocolate biscuits, no less! We'll be *very* welcome upstairs! Come along and let's do what we can to get that worried look off your face. It doesn't suit your peculiar style of beauty at all, let me tell you! "

Hilda Annersley gave it up and laughed. "You are always you, Nell! Well, if you've quite finished rifling my cupboard, we may as well go. I'll bring the biscuits!"

Nell Wilson joined in her laughter. "Yes; you look more like your usual bonny self now! Lead on, Macduff! "

They went up the flight of stairs just outside the study door, turned down a short passage and ended up outside a door from which came the sound of voices.

"They seem to be enjoying a barney," Miss Wilson murmured. "In you go! "

Miss Annersley opened the door just as Miss Moore, the geography mistress, was proclaiming loudly, "The only one who has done any work worthy of the name is Margot Maynard and she has one of her trying fits on and goodness knows how long *that* may last! "

"*Who* is being trying?" demanded the Head who had missed the first part of the sentence. She and Miss Wilson walked in and shut the door behind them. "We've come to have coffee with you if we may. We've brought our cups and saucers *and*," impressively, "a box of chocolate biscuits. May we stay?"

"With all the pleasure in life! " exclaimed Biddy O'Ryan, the history mistress. "There are two chairs in this corner shrieking to be occupied. Come and sit down, and give me your cups. Mdlle's officiating as usual."

The pair sat down and she went to the table where Mdlle de Lachennais, head of the languages staff, was pouring out coffee. Meanwhile, Miss Annersley had tumbled her biscuits on to a plate proffered by Nancy Wilmot, the maths mistress, and people were helping themselves gratefully.

The Head thanked Miss O'Ryan for her coffee and turned to Miss Moore.

"And now, Rosalind, tell me: who were you accusing of being trying?"

"No, I didn't mean it in that sense," Miss Moore said. "At least, almost the whole of Upper IVb are enough to vex a saint; but as I used it then about young Margot, I meant that she was trying her best—and succeeding."

"I'm very glad to hear it. But Margot has done really better this past year—ever since she fell into Lake Lucerne, in fact. What is the matter with the rest?"

"General wickedness! " This was Miss Derwent, the senior English mistress. "The holidays seem to have upset the few brains most of them can boast. I propose to have them for the first hour tomorrow for the purpose of instill-

45

ing a few facts about the analysis of English sentences into their heads. But," impressively, "I shall make an exception of Margot who got two-thirds of her work right."

Miss Andrews, who took junior English, looked up. "But tomorrow's your Free, Ruth, and you said you were going to Berne."

"I know it. But I am conscientious. Those young monkeys can't be left to think they can get away with anything as awful as the analysis they handed in this morning. It's their free hour and they're going to lose it. And that, I hope, will make them all think a little!"

"I know; but what I set out to say is that I'm taking Lower IVa for analysis at that time and if you like to send your beauties to me, I'll take them, too."

Miss Derwent's face, which had been clouded at the thought of losing her trip, brightened considerably. "Would you? Oh, Sharlie, I'd be everlastingly grateful! If you want to know, I've an appointment with Herr Albrecht —a back tooth that's been twingeing warningly. And," she added with a deep chuckle, "it would teach those little wretches a lesson. They won't like having to go down to Lower for a lesson one little bit."

"That, they certainly will *not*!" Miss Moore, who was form mistress to the young ladies under discussion, spoke with great emphasis. "Furthermore, it should ram well home what I told them in geography this morning."

"What was that?" Five people joined in the question.

"That if I had much more trouble with them, I should ask Rosalie to rearrange the timetable so that they should go down to Lower for a full week. I don't know what's got into them this term, but they seem to have returned in a state of blank ignorance so far as *my* subject is concerned."

Miss Annersley look meditative. Miss Wilson gave her a wicked look and said gently, "I could complain about my botany lessons with them, likewise. Hilda, those young demons need a lesson. We're all here. What about getting together over the timetable and doing as Rosalind suggests?"

"I've no objection," her friend said. "I can't complain myself. They know better than to try to play me up. I'm rather surprised they dare do it with you, Nell. What's happened to your renowned sarcastic tongue?"

Miss Wilson, whose gift for sarcasm was famed throughout the school, smiled sweetly. "They had a good dose of it this morning. By the time I'd finished with them, five were weeping copiously and some of the others weren't far from it. Margot Maynard, Isabel Drew and Nan Wentworth were the only three who escaped."

"Yes; spare Nan, all of you." Miss Annersley looked round them. "She isn't a clever child, I know, but with her medical history—or rather her family's—the more lightly we ride her at present, the better."

They nodded and Miss Moore went back to the original suggestion. "Well, with the exception of Margot—it won't hurt Nan to go down for a week—are you all agreed that Upper IVb and Lower IVa are to work together for a week?" she demanded.

They were. All the junior mistresses and one or two of the senior had been suffering from the antics of Upper IVb and they were not sorry that they should get their deserts.

"Well, you'll have to arrange your timetable among you," Miss Dene warned them, "I'm altering it for no one. It's a violent headache at the end of every summer holiday and change it all round just for one week, I *will not*! Take either their own or Lower IVa's and let it go at that. It'll give some of you a little time off to be thinking about your year-end exams paper which I want in by half-term to get them duplicated," she added kindly.

"Why is it that that age is always the outside of enough?" Nancy Wilmot wanted to know. "I remember when I was a prefect, it was always that age that nearly drove us crackers. And," she added cheerfully, "I seem to remember being a fearful pest myself about then."

Miss Wilson laughed. "It's always the same. The fact of the matter is they've outgrown the small-girl stage and aren't quite old enough to have developed sense. I remember Joey and Co. at twelve-thirteen and a more outrageous set of young sinners, I never want to encounter. Don't worry, Nancy. Most of them will have begun to develop a sense of responsibility by next year. By that time, of course,

47

we shall have Enid Matthews and Co. taking their places as the school's worst worriers. However, that wasn't what we came to consult you about."

"I thought there was a catch in it," Biddy O'Ryan said suspiciously. "What's the latest worry?"

"This letter." Miss Annersley produced it and handed it to Mdlle as the doyenne of the staff. "Yes; you may all read it. I want your advice."

Mdlle read it and passed it on to the cluster of younger mistresses who left it to Miss Derwent to read aloud.

"Well, whoever Herbert William Baker may be, he doesn't give you much information about his grand-daughter," she commented when she had finished. "Do you want us to say whether we think you ought to take her? Because it strikes me as a chancy thing. This girl mayn't know the first thing about languages and we have bother enough with Rosamund Lilley that way. I had to repeat one sentence in German seven times on Friday before she got the sense of it—and *then* it was only because Len Maynard helped her out. If we have *two* like that in one form, my hair will be white by the end of term!"

"How is it that Rosamund knows nothing of even French?" Biddy asked.

"She came to us from a school where it wasn't taught," the Head replied. "The Gays sent her and Mrs. Gay told me that she knew no languages but her own. But she does try, Ruth. By the end of term, she should be able to manage as well as most of them."

"Do you know," Miss Wilson put in solemnly, "I foresee a frightful muddle ahead of us next term when it comes to arranging the new forms. You *can't* have children of twelve in any Fifth and yet it won't be fair to keep either Len or Con down in even Upper IVa."

Rosalie Dene laughed. "Don't worry! I've been con-sidering that point already. We are going to have an inter-mediate form—the Shell, in fact—and Len and Con will both go into it. So will Maeve Bettany and some others. We have three or four girls who oughtn't to be pushed; and girls like Jo Scott who will be as well for another year at—well—intermediate work before they tackle the definitely senior work of a Fifth."

"How shall we manage for staff?" Biddy asked. "Sure, we've a hard enough time as it is, fitting everything in."

"We're having another mistresss," Miss Annersley told her briskly. "And apart from that, Joey's new Help is going to take on some of the work with junior languages."

"Oh, has she got one?" Nancy Wilmot cried. "Who is it—anyone we know?"

"Yes," Miss Annersley's eyes danced. "I think you all know her—all who are Old Girls, at any rate. *You* know her very well, Mdlle."

"Vraiment?" Mdlle's black eyes sparkled. "But Hilda, chérie, I know so many—but so very many of the Old Girls. Which is she?"

"Go back to Tirol days and think."

"But that is very far back," Mdlle laughed. "Ah, well! Let me consider!"

But before she had time, Nancy Wilmot was on her feet. "I've got it—Maria Marani! She always used to say she would like to teach languages only first there was all that ghastly business with Herr Marani and then later they went to America to join Gisela and Gottfried. But I had a letter from Maria at Christmas and she said Gottfried had sold his practice and was coming back to Innsbruck now that Herr Mensch was dead. Oh, is Gottfried joining San up here? He *is*!" as the Head nodded. "How simply marvellous! And Maria is going to Joey? Well, that's wizard news! I only wish Bernhilda and Kurt would follow their example and come, too."

"So they are. Kurt's firm have recalled him to take charge of their branch in Berne and they're coming in the autumn. Frieda is trying to find a house for them. With their long family, a flat won't be much good."

"How many have they?"

"Seven now. Of course, Bernhilda's youngest, Hilda, is nine now; but they are all at home except Natalie, the eldest. She is twenty and has trained as a nurse—is training, I should say. She will come to San, too."

"Well, it's all very nice," Miss Wilson put in practically, "but we've side-tracked miles from the problem of this proposed new girl. Can't any of you think of something?"

"I suggest," Mdlle said, "that Rosalie should send a

prospectus and ask in her letter if the girl cannot wait until the Christmas term. Meanwhile, she can also ask her name, age, and capabilities. At least let us know so much."

The rest acclaimed this solution and it was decided on. Then the staff decided to call it a day, so the session ended and Rosalie Dene was instructed to send the prospectus and letter next day. Until the reply came to that, no more could be done about the school's latest problem.

CHAPTER VI

SHOCK FOR ROSAMUND

ROSAMUND had not been at the Chalet School two days before she had discovered that one of the most important of the elder girls was Mary-Lou Trelawney. Mary-Lou proved to be a member of Upper V and all school prefects belonged to either Upper or Lower VI. She was a House Prefect, of course; but then, so were Janet Overton and Bess Appleton and it certainly didn't make them important in the same way as Mary-Lou.

"What *is* it?" she asked of Len Maynard one day; but Len was no more able to explain than she was and they had to wait till they met Joey Maynard wheeling Cecil out for her morning walk, with Mike and the twins racing in front of her, to get an answer.

Upper IVa should have been having tennis, but a regrettable accident to the courts they should have been using—the sudden swelling of a tiny stream under the influence of a whole night's downpour of rain—had made that impossible. The courts were under three inches of water and until it drained off, no one could do much about it. Therefore, the Head had decreed a ramble instead so long as they didn't ramble off the paths.

The stream was normally a ditch, but the folk of the Görnetz Platz had known for centuries what to expect and a rude but sturdy bridge crossed it at one point. Upper IVa, returning from their ramble, saw Mrs. Maynard trundling the pram at the far side and waited.

Mike, who was going through a phase of manly scorn

for girls, grinned at them and went on in a lordly way, followed by Felix, who was his shadow at this period. Felicity paused beside her elder sisters, however, to chatter eagerly. She was a sprite-like small person, with flaxen curls bobbing gaily all over her small head and her sister Margot's forget-me-not blue eyes dancing under the brown brows and long curling lashes.

Len and Con hugged her and they talked fast. Then Len said, "You go on talking to Con, Felicity. Rosamund, come with me. I want to ask Miss Wilmot something."

This being Friday and German day, she spoke in German. Rosamund knew by this time what "Komm mit mir" meant. The rest she had to guess at. They went up to where the escort mistress was standing waving to Joey to cross the bridge first and Len put her request.

"Please, may Rosamund and I go on and speak to Mamma? There is something I wish to ask her."

Nancy Wilmot grinned. "Is this a way of having an extra peep at Cecil?" she asked in her fluent German.

Len shook her chestnut head. "Oh, no! We really do want to ask her something. May we go, Miss Wilmot?"

"Very well—but only for three minutes. I'll time you from—now!" And Miss Wilmot turned up her wrist.

Len gave a faint shriek of dismay, grabbed Rosamund's hand and raced her across the bridge to where Joey was standing, beckoning to the ramble to cross first. She smiled broadly at the pair and ceased her gestures. "Hello! What's the why of this?"

"Please, Mamma," Len said, still speaking in German, "we have only three minutes. Can you tell us why Mary-Lou is so important?"

Joey gasped. "In three minutes or less? No; certainly not! It couldn't be done. But," she added, "I'll ring up and ask if you three and Rosamund may come to us for Kaffee und Kuchen on Sunday and I'll try to help you then." She smiled at Rosamund who was peeping in the pram. "Want to see our baby, Rosamund? Just a peep, then." And she drew back the pink pram cover to show the little dark head lying on the pillow. Cecil was asleep, but Rosamund was delighted with the smooth peachy skin and the very long black lashes curling against it.

"Oh, what a darling! " she exclaimed fervently.

"In German please! " Mrs. Maynard said with mock severity. "Isn't this German day? Very well, then. Do you know how to say it? No? Right! I'll tell you! Repeat it after me. 'Sie ist ein Liebling!' Got that? Then say it. Len, you see that she learns it by heart. Actually, Rosamund, that means, 'She is a darling' but it'll do you. Take every chance, my lamb, of picking up words and phrases. The more you do that, the sooner you'll find you can manage," she went on, speaking in English now. "I mean it. And now, we must get on. Goodness knows where those two imps, Mike and Felix, are by this time. And if I hold you folk up much longer, you'll be most appallingly late for whatever it is comes next. I'll see you all on Sunday, D.V., and we can talk then. I'll push on and you wait here for the others. Good-bye!" She beamed at them and pushed the pram forward. Len and Rosamund said "Auf Wiedersehen" and waited till the rest crossed the bridge after the girls had had as much of a peep as they could manage at the pram's contents. Joey refused to linger, and she called Felicity to leave Con and come at once, and went on towards the pretty chalet rented for the present by Sir Guy and Lady Rutherford, cousins of Nina Rutherford of Vb, and here because their eldest girl, Alix, was at the big Sanatorium at the other end of the Platz.

"The brook's running full," Len said, hanging over the edge of the bridge to look at it.

"Ich verstehe nicht," Rosamund said with a good British accent. She knew *that* one, anyhow, having to say it about a hundred times every German day.

Len gave her the translation and then made her repeat it until the rest were beside them. Miss Wilmot came last and she laughed as they joined the end of the crocodile.

"Did you get what you wanted?" she queried.

"No; but Mamma is going to ask if we three and Rosamund may go to Kaffee und Kuchen with her on Sunday and then she'll explain," Len said. "She said she couldn't possibly do it in three minutes."

Rosamund looked at her enviously as Miss Wilmot nodded and laughed again before she hurried on to direct the long line. "I wish," she said in laborious German, "that I could talk like you."

Len answered her slowly and clearly. "But I do not know when I did not speak both German and French," she said. "You try hard, Rosamund, and you will find that you are speaking quite well by the end of term. Didn't Mamma tell you you would find it easy if you tried to learn every time you heard new words or phrases?" Rosamund understood perhaps half of this; but Len stuck to it, explaining odd words here and there until, by the time they had reached the school, the new girl could feel that she had learnt quite a little on the ramble.

The next day it pleased Katharine Gordon, the Games prefect, to take advantage of the fact that the brook had returned to normal proportions and begin the job of selecting the various Tennis Sixes. The courts were mainly en tout cas or asphalt and they could do without the two grass courts which were still mud's own self.

As soon as Elevenses was over the girls carried out the benches they used and settled themselves comfortably to watch and comment. This being Saturday they spoke English so, except for the comparatively few French, Swiss and German girls, language was no obstacle. The Maynard triplets took advantage of the fact that you could sit where you liked and crowded together with Rosamund between Len and Con and Margot's own special chum, Emerence Hope, at her far side. Len looked rather wistfully at her great friend, Prunella Davidson, but Prunella was with a group of Vb girls and though she waved to Len, it was not to be expected that she would leave her own peers just now. It was very difficult to see much of each other now that Prunella was a Senior, so Len was glad Rosamund seemed to be fitting in with her.

Until they went to Canada the triplets had stuck together. But Margot had been sent off with her aunt, Lady Russell, a year before the others came and that had made the first break. Since then, although Con the dreamer seemed more or less content with her own family, both Len and Margot had branched out. Margot had chummed with one of the naughtiest girls the school had ever known, and Len, after nearly two years of general friendliness, had chummed up with Prunella Davidson.

Len gave a tiny sigh and then settled down to watching the tennis. She touched Rosamund's arm and murmured, "You watch hard. You can pick up no end of tips just by watching good players and the people who are playing today are among the best we have."

"Here come the first four!" Margot interrupted her. "Mary-Lou, Hilary, Carola and Bess. It's Mary-Lou and Carola against the other pair. *Now* we'll see something!"

"Is Mary-Lou playing?" Emerence asked. "Oh, good!"

Rosamund noticed that her eyes shone and wondered about it. Later she was to learn that Mary-Lou's accident had been caused by Emerence's deliberate disobedience and that young lady had had a shock from which she had not fully recovered though it was nearly six months ago.[1]

The two pairs were evenly matched. Mary-Lou played an excellent game and big Carola, while she was lacking in style, forced the pace considerably with her slashing returns. Hilary Wilson, a prefect, placed her balls well and Bess played a good game on the whole.

"That's deuce called for the third time!" Con exclaimed after a fiery rally had ended in favour of Mary-Lou and Carola. "Mary-Lou's playing awfully well, Len. She wasn't nearly so good last summer."

"No; she and Carola have Hilary and Bess well on the run," Len agreed, watching them critically. "I think Mary-Lou is safe for one of the pairs, don't you?"

"So long as her back doesn't play her up—or her head," Con assented; and Emerence went scarlet and fidgeted.

"Nyerts to that!" Margot retorted. "There was never much wrong with her back but bruises and as soon as they cleared up, *that* was all right. And I should say her head's good, too. You can bet if there'd been anything to fuss about *Matey* would have pitched in. But she's over there with the rest of the staff and not doing a thing about it."

"Oh, well-played, Hilary!" Len exclaimed, clapping hard as Hilary made a wild leap upwards and just got her racquet to a skied return of Carola's, smashing it over to Mary-Lou's side where that wary young woman leapt

[1] Mary-Lou of the Chalet School.

back, caught it and drove it hard over to Bess who took it on the edge of her racquet, sending it well out. "Vantage striker! It's Carola's service and she serves like a man. I wouldn't like to be Bess!"

That seemed to be what Bess herself thought, for the service, low, swift and with all Carola's force behind it, completely beat her and the trial was over. The four players straggled up to the net and shook hands and then left the court, laughing and chattering, while four more people came on for the five games that constituted the test. It ended sooner than the first, for Vi Lucy and Sybil Russell were easily outplayed by Sally Winslow and Jill Ormsby. There was half an hour left before the bell would ring for them to wash before Mittagessen and Miss Burnett, the games mistress, stepped forward to announce that the time would be given to an exhibition game between Blossom Willoughby and Katharine Gordon. The two prefects responsible for the games appeared on the court and Janice Willoughby and Ailie Russell, who were acting as ball boys, ran forward with a net of new balls.

"Now you really *will* see something!" Len informed her new friend. "Miss Burnett says that some day Katharine ought to play for England. She's a marvel. And Blossom was nearly as good at the end of last summer. I know Katharine stayed with the Willoughbys last hols and they had some practice on their hard court."

The game began and Rosamund watching carefully, helped thereto by the comments the other four muttered at intervals, began to see what she meant. The others had been quite good for schoolgirls, especially Mary-Lou and Carola, but they lacked the style and judgment shown by both Katharine and Blossom. What she saw filled her with longing to play like that.

"I'll never do it, though," she said aloud sadly.

"Never do what?" Con asked amazedly.

"Play like that. Oh, just *look* at that one!" as a return from Katharine skimmed low over the net to land dead at Blossom's feet. "Blossom never had a chance at it!"

Mary-Lou and Co. had come to sit beside their juniors, that being the only reasonably clear place, and Mary-Lou overheard. She bent across Len with a grin to remark,

"That's pure wiliness! Katt Gordon's a whizzer at that sort of thing. She plays with her head as well as all the rest of her. Shove up a little and make room for a little 'un, you folk! Change places with Rosamund, will you, Len. I want to explain a bit to Rosamund. If she's so keen, she can learn a lot just watching this."

"Oh, good! Just what I wanted!" And Len beamed.

Then followed an exposition of the strokes that helped Rosamund far more than the swift remarks of Miss Burnett during games times.

"There she goes! Watch her follow right through, Rosamund. See! Her racquet and her whole body finished right in line—Oh, well taken, Blossom!" as Blossom took the ball plumb in the centre of her racquet and drove steadily down the court.

Katharine had never taken her eye off the ball and she sprang across and returned it. A sharp rally followed, both players volleying until Katharine saw her chance and suddenly drove into the far corner with a swift drive which beat Blossom and lost her the point.

The service which followed was a nasty one—low, swift and breaking in. Blossom just managed to return it and Katharine, waiting at net, smashed it down and it broke right out, giving her the game by two points.

It was Blossom's turn to serve, and Mary-Lou called Rosamund's attention to her position, "Look; that's the way to stand—right shoulder back *and* right foot. Now watch how her racquet follows the ball. You've got to do that or the ball loses pace and direction. See!"

The service was over, low, swift and straight. Katharine returned it neatly to the far corner, but Blossom was watching and she was there to return it—a nasty return, just lipping over the net and trickling down the other side. Katharine tried to take it but it was untakable and she lost the point. However, there was no mistake about the next and her return broke out instead of in as everyone, including Blossom herself, had expected.

"That's a nasty return," Mary-Lou said critically. "Wonder how she gets that screw on the ball? I must find out. That's fifteen all. Blossom's come on a lot since last summer, hasn't she, Hilary?"

Hilary Wilson nodded. "She's always been good. She plays a lot at home with her father. That's why her service is so fierce for a girl. But she's got a lot wilier and that's what she needed. Oh, glory! Look at Katharine! Her back-stroke is as strong as the forward. That's where I fail. My backhand is weak and always has been."

"You don't get the right stance," Mary-Lou said absently as she watched a sharp rally. "You've *got* to have your right shoulder forward or you go all over the shop."

Rosamund noted this and decided that the next time she was sent to the practice board, she would see what she could do about it. So far, she had only patted the ball straight against it. But that morning's work had filled her with a fresh ambition. She doubted if she could ever be as good as either Katharine or Blossom. But she would certainly do her best to reach Hilary's standard at least; and she would give particular care to her backhand.

A clever drive from Katharine beat Blossom at that point. She did manage to reach the ball, but only just and she returned it feebly into the net. The score now stood at thirty-forty, and a minute later Katharine's return to Blossom's service gave her the game.

The first bell rang then and they had to give it up and go to the Splasheries to wash their hands and tidy generally for Mittagessen. But during the meal nothing much was talked but tennis, and when they had had their rest they all streamed out to the courts again to watch tests between other girls. The afternoon ended with Mary-Lou, Carola and two other girls, Elinor Pennell, who played a very pretty game, making up by cunning what she lacked in strength, and Lalla Winterton who was a good all-round player being chosen for the match pairs. The others cheered the decision loudly and Miss Burnett led the applause. The reserves must be left till another time, for there were several girls all at the same standard more or less and the mistress announced that they would be tried one evening next week for selection.

The girls went to fetch out their crockery and food, for, as long as they made no trouble for anyone else, they might have Kaffee und Kuchen in the garden if the weather was fine. After the meal they would go in and change into their evening frocks, ready for the Saturday Evening which was in charge of the two Sixths today. They had arranged for a series of paper games and quiet competitions. They were to be heard in Hall dragging tables and chairs into place and laughing and talking as they worked.

Rosamund, pulling straight the pretty green frock of silky material Mrs. Gay had chosen for her, reflected that it was as well she had decided on the diary idea. There would be any amount to add to her home letter without going into school details in it. She brushed out her silky dark hair and tied it loosely back from her face with a broad green ribbon. Then, after a glance in her mirror to make sure that all was well, she tidied up her cubicle, removed and folded her counterpane when the dormitory door opened and Matron arrived.

"Rosamund Lilley!" she called.

Rosamund stepped out between the curtains, a startled look on her face. "I'm here, Matron," she said.

"Oh, good! Changed? Let me look at you. Got a clean handkerchief? Cubicle tidy? Let me see!" She came to the cubicle and looked round. "Yes; very nice. Right! Then run away down to the study. Miss Annersley wants you for a moment." And she left the room, followed by Rosamund wondering why she was wanted.

Matron turned right to go to her own room and Rosamund had to go down the stairs at the other end. She ran down, holding her lengthy tail of hair to keep it tidy. Another minute and she was tapping at the door of the study. The Head's voice bade her enter and she went in, remembering in time to make the curtsy to the Head that was considered de rigeur at the Chalet School. As she rose she looked up and then she nearly stumbled and fell. Standing by the desk, grinning triumphantly at her, was the last person in the world that she had expected to see—as she knew in a flash, that she *wanted* to see.

Miss Annersley smiled at her and said, "There you are, Rosamund. Joan Baker has come to join us and she tells me you two know each other. She is in Tulip dormitory. Will you take her there and ask Elinor Pennell to show her her cubicle? Then run down to Hall, and when Joan has changed Elinor will bring her down and you can look after her until she finds her feet. Thank you, dear. Go with her, Joan."

Stunned to silence by the shock, Rosamund curtsied again and led the way out, Joan following. But when the door was shut behind them, the newest of the new girls turned to her former friend and said, "Aha, Rosamund Lilley! You didn't expect this, did you? But when Dad said I was to go to a decent school, I told him I wanted to go to yours. Your old frosty-face of a Head made a lot of difficulty, but she had to give up in the end. Money always talks, Dad says. So here I am and you're to take care of me and mind you do or I'll have something to say. Where's this dormitory they talk of? Lead the way."

Rosamund had got her breath by the time she ran down. Turning to the stairs, she simply said, "We aren't allowed to talk on the stairs and passages. We go down here. Tulip is on the floor above Marigold where I sleep. But Elinor will look after you all right."

Joan gave her a sharp look as she led the way and her eyes narrowed. This new school had done something to Ros Lilley. She wasn't quite the same girl. Perhaps it wasn't going to be so easy as she had imagined to get her under her thumb again. Oh, well, Joan felt sure that a few hints of all she could say about young Ros's home and people would soon put an end to that. Judging this school by the ones of which she had read in the cheap weeklies, she thought the other girls wouldn't be eager to be friends with a girl whose father was only a worker in a market garden and whose mother had been a housemaid. She smiled to herself as she followed Rosamund along the passage and up the two flights of stairs to the dormitory where Elinor Pennell, a prefect and a member of VIb, was breathlessly changing after helping to bring Hall to order for the evening and felt none too pleased at having to take on a new girl at this hour of the day.

CHAPTER VII

A SATURDAY EVENING

HAVING handed Joan over to Elinor, Rosamund made straight for Hall where she ran into Mary-Lou, tall and capable-looking in her frock of thin woolly material in a shade of blue that exactly matched her very blue eyes. Her short crop of light brown curls had been burnished until they gleamed in the evening light. She had at one time been a sturdy, rather squareset creature, but her illness before Christmas had changed that and now she was slim though there was nothing of lankiness about her. That illness together with her early life spent among older people had made her in some ways very grown-up for her age. Rosamund, looking up to apologise for bumping into her, had a sudden feeling that here was someone who could advise her. After all these weeks of being away from Joan's influence as well as being plunged into an entirely new atmosphere, she knew all at once that even when she had been most under Joan's thumb, there had been things about the girl she had never liked.

"And Mum and Dad didn't like her at all!" she thought even as she said, "Oh, I'm awfully sorry. I didn't mean to barge into you like that."

Mary-Lou grinned. "Didn't see me, I suppose. I should have said there was rather a lot of me to overlook!"

As she was nearly five foot eight in height, this was true and might have sounded snubbing, but there was nothing of the snub in the way in which it was said and Rosamund smiled shyly back at her. The blue eyes were keen, however, and Mary-Lou was nothing if not sympathetic. She had been on her way to hunt for Verity Carey, but she paused to inquire, "Anything wrong with you?"

"I—no; nothing, thank you," Rosamund stammered.

"Rot!" Mary-Lou spoke with emphasis. "Something's happened since we went up to change. Then your one idea was to emulate Katt Gordon's tennis exploits and you were bubbling over with keenness. Now you look as if the cat had eaten your canary. Anything I can do to help?"

This chimed so exactly with Rosamund's thoughts that she literally jumped. "H-how did you know? How—what do you mean?" she asked quickly.

"Exactly what I say," quoth Mary-Lou. "Look here, Rosamund, I don't want to butt in on your private affairs, of course, but if there's anything wrong—now or at any other time—and you think I can help, come and ask me." She paused, and then she added, "I know you're by way of being pally with Len Maynard, but she's only a kid, and younger than you. Come to me if you want me. Or better still, when you've got to know her as you *will*, go to Aunt Jocy—I mean Mrs. Maynard. She may be the proud Ma of a long family, but in some ways she stays around our age and she understands better than any grown-up I've ever known."

"Is she your aunt?" Rosamund queried, surprised. "I didn't know."

"Not really. It's an adoptive relationship. Verity and I always call her that and so do a good many other folk. The Lucys, for example, and the Chesters. She's always ready to help if she can and though she isn't in the school now, yet she *is* at the same time. See what I mean?"

The fine confusion of her statement might have bewildered most folk, but Rosamund saw what she was driving at and nodded. "I understand, I think. Thanks awfully for saying *you'll* help me out if I need it. I can't say anything just now, but something's happened and it's just possible I may need advice. If I can come to you if it gets beyond me it'll be an awful help."

"O.K.; you can. And while I think of it, find another adjective or someone will be down on you for calling everything 'awful', whether it is or not," Mary-Lou said with another of her friendly grins. "That's all? Then I must go and rout out that ghastly sister-by-marriage of mine, Verity Carey. Her dad married Mother you know, and that's the nearest relationship we can come to. Verity's the most awful mooner—worse than Con Maynard. It's a hard life at times, but I'm accustomed to it now!" With which philosophic reflection she nodded and went off and Rosamund looked round for Len and Co.

They were at the far side of the room and Len was waving frantically at her. Rosamund made her way round the sides—and discovered that they were seated at a table for four—Len, Con and Betty Landon. Margot, and her boon companion Emerence Hope, sat at the next and both grinned a welcome to her. Between all this and Mary-Lou's unexpected offer to help, Rosamund's spirits rose and the worried look faded out of her face.

"Come on!" Len said. "We've had a terrific time keeping your place. Bag your chair and be quick."

The worried look came back. "It's sweet of you all but I don't know if I *can*. There's a new girl just come today and I knew her before. We used to go to the same school. She told the Head and she said I was to look after her for the present. Perhaps I'd better go somewhere where there's room for two. I'm awf—I mean," as Mary-Lou's warning came back to her, "*very* sorry, Len."

Betty was a good-natured girl. She jumped up at once. "Don't talk bilge! I'll join Alicia. Then you can have the new girl here. What's her name, by the way?"

"Joan Baker. Oh, Betty, do you mind awf—fearfully?"

"Of course I don't! We're to play progressive games, Jean Ackroyd says, and that means that we'll be moving on every ten minutes or so. See you later, I expect!" And she went off gaily to make up Alicia Leonard's table.

Con Maynard might be, as Mary-Lou had said, a mooner, but now and then she startled people by showing herself very keen-eyed. Now she said, "Don't you like her —the new girl, I mean? You don't seem very pleased."

"I used to but I haven't seen her for some time," Rosamund replied carefully.

Len kicked her sister under the table and Con subsided.

"I wonder just what we are going to do?" the eldest Maynard remarked when she saw that Con understood. "They've given us these folded slips and pencils so it's a paper game of some kind. Margot and Emmy have to thread needles. Isn't it awful?"

"You bet I wouldn't have sat down here if I'd known,"

said Emerence herself gloomily. "Oh, well! I may get moved by being worst! You never know!"

"Do you like paper games?" Margot asked with a giggle. "We love them. We often play them at home."

"I don't think I know any—except Consequences."

"That's fun," Con chuckled, "but we know lots of others. Remember last time we played Book Reviews, Len?"

Len gave a peal of laughter. "Don't I just! You mean the one which went: 'Ker-splash! Did She Fall or Was She Pushed?' That really was a yell! 'Specially the review at the end about it being a book with a sound moral!'"

Rosamund was interested. "How do you play it?" she asked.

"Oh, you begin with the title of a book. You make it up. Then you fold it over and pass it on and write a sub-title: Like 'Eric; or Little by Little'. Then you give the author. Then you give two reviews with *their* authors and then you read it out. It's a complete yell sometimes!"

"And then there's the Picture game," Con began.

She got no further, for at that moment, Elinor came into the room, very dainty in her coral-pink frock with her dark hair swung round her head in smooth plaits. Behind her came Joan, and Joan's idea of a semi-evening frock was a bright scarlet jersey-cloth heavily braided in black and far too old-looking for a schoolgirl. Her hair had been artificially waved and crinkled over her head in stiff waves. She wore a large cameo brooch which swore at the red of her dress and a string of red beads. She was also powdered and lip-sticked in a way that had made Elinor nearly gasp aloud. The Seniors at the Chalet School might use a dust of powder and even a little pink lipstick on state occasions, but it had to be properly applied. The prefect had said nothing at the time, thinking it wiser to leave the matter to the staff. *They* would soon put a stop to it. Only girls of sixteen or over might use make-up at all and Elinor guessed that Joan Baker was nowhere near that yet. Rosamund, getting up reluctantly to go and bring her to their table, looked far younger.

Elinor smiled at her. "Joan tells me the Head has asked you to take charge of her for the present," she said in her clear-cut, well-bred voice. "Hope you'll enjoy the evening,

Joan. Rosamund will look after you as far as she can, I know." She nodded pleasantly at the pair and then went off for Betsy Lucy was frantically signalling to her that it was time that the evening's entertainment began.

"We're over there," Rosamund said to Joan. "Come along. I've kept a place for you."

She led the way and Joan followed her, looking round curiously as she went. She despised the pretty girlish frocks worn by all the others and told herself complacently that she was much the smartest there. When they came to the table where the two eldest Maynards were sitting, she looked scornful. They were so clearly mere kids! As for that Pennell girl with her lad-di-dah voice and manners, Joan felt that she would like to say or do something really vulgar to knock her off her perch. And here was young Ros cultivating just that kind of voice! And here Joan had to stop short for Rosamund had always spoken prettily and all that was happening was that she was beginning to lose her Hampshire accent.

They had reached the table by this time, and Rosamund said simply, "Len and Con, this is Joan Baker. Joan, these are Len and Con Maynard." She glanced at the other table, but Sybil Russell and Clare Kennedy had come there and were laughing and talking with Margot and Emerence, so she let it go, saw that Joan was settled and then turned as the bell on the Head's desk on the platform rang and Betsy Lucy gave out instructions.

"You have ten minutes for each game," she said. "When the bell rings, you stop and after whoever is responsible for your table has checked up, you move on. The winner from each table goes forward, the loser back. The other two stay where they are and have another shot. The members of the two Sixths—except Sybil who is playing to make the numbers even—will tell you what to do each time. The games begin—*Now!*"

At once everyone started in. At Rosamund's table, when they had opened their folded slips, they found them headed with a large N and beneath a list, Country, Town, River, Book Title, Girl's Name, Boy's Name. They had to name one of each beginning with the letter N.

"Keep them as out of the ordinary as you can," Len

warned the others. "If you get names other people have, they're crossed out and won't count."

The two Maynards and Rosamund concentrated on the work which wasn't easy. It is odd, but in things like this, everything you want to remember so often seems to slip out of your mind. Joan, yawning ostentatiously, scribbled in a few names here and there. Then she gave it up and occupied herself with staring around.

Len finished first. She folded her list and looked at the others. Con was still scribbling hard, but Rosamund, having stuck at the river, gave it up with a sigh, folded her slip and handed it to Len.

"I've done all I can," she said. "You'd better have them all to hand in. Have you finished, Joan?"

"Done!" said Con triumphantly. "Here's mine, Len. You'd best take them till someone comes along——"

"I've come," said Betsy Lucy's voice behind her. "Finished, all of you? Hand them over, Len."

She took them, skimmed through them rapidly, crossing out lines here and there, and nodded. "O.K. Len, you go forward and you—Joan Baker, isn't it?—go back. You and Rosamund remain, Con. Here; take charge of the next lists and give them out when the bell rings. New letter this time. Mind you don't peep!" she added, laughing as she went on to the next table.

"I wonder what it is?" Con said. "Isn't N an awful letter? I was nearly stuck over the book, but I put *Nicholas Nickleby*, I don't suppose it'll be much help to me."

"It was the only one I could think of," Rosamund acknowledged. "And what river begins with N? I couldn't think of one!"

"I put the Neister," Con said.

Len exclaimed. "Goodness, Con! Had you forgotten it's spelt with a D at the beginning? I put the Nen." She turned politely to Joan, "What did you get?

"Oh, give it a miss," Joan said with another yawn. "Is this the best you can do in the evenings? I sh'd have thought you'd have danced. Not much fun without boys, of course, but it 'ud be better than playing baby games. I just didn't bother." She picked up the slips. "Like me to tell you the letter? That wouldn't be peeping."

"You can't do that!" Con said in shocked tones. "It would be cheating!"

"Oh, raspberries to that! It doesn't matter."

"Yes, it does!" Rosamund said, sharply. "We're playing for prizes. And anyhow, we can't cheat, whatever it is!"

"Oh, I quite forgot. Our little Rosamund is such a *good* girl! Never peeps or does anything of that kind! You're too pi to live, Ros Lilley!" She caught Len Maynard's eye and stopped short, for there was unfeigned horror in the younger girl's face. "Oh, don't look like that, young 'un! Can't you see a joke when you meet it?"

Luckily for everyone, the bell rang then and the pair of them had to move—Len to do what she could with the KATE game, and Joan to thread needles, while Hilda Jukes moved back and lovely Sybil Russell came forward to join Rosamund and Con and do what they could with the letter S. This time, Rosamund moved forward and Hilda went back to thread needles which she did with despatch and had to return to LISTS from which this time, she contrived to escape after a round with the letter L.

Taken all round, the Seniors had shown a good deal of ingenuity. Shrieks of horror came from the people who had to pick up peas with a pair of knitting needles and put them into a cup. Most folk failed ignominiously to manage more than two or three, though Verity Carey distinguished herself with a total of seven. Nina Rutherford got every name in the BOOK WEDDING correct. A round of CORINTHIAN BAGATELLE brought laurels to Margot Maynard, and Rosamund won the TOUCHING competition by long odds.

WEIGHT GUESSING proved a snare and a delusion to most folk who made the maddest guesses at the six objects given them. As for CRYPTOGRAMS, which consisted of disentangling twelve geographical terms whose letters had been well and truly muddled, most folk retired with a bare half attempted. As Hilary Bennet said, what are you to make of TSWREAEDH and IEOSCSR?

Halfway through the evening Betsy once more mounted the platform and requested everyone to stay where she was when the next bell rang, and the two Sixths brought round trays laden with sandwiches, plates of jelly and blancmange and dishes of ripe gooseberries contributed by Joey Maynard. These dainties were accompanied by cups of hot chocolate and whipped cream and were greatly appreciated by everyone. The idea also meant that a bare twenty minutes was spent over Abendessen and then they went on with their games.

At half-past twenty the Head took the platform and told them that the present round was the last and winners would be announced at the end. While the girls did their best, Hilary Wilson and Blossom Willoughby brought in a table laden with tiny prizes and the winners were called out to receive their rewards. They consisted of lavender or potpourri bags, gay little handkerchiefs, bars of chocolate and needlebooks. A wise rule in the school said that no group might spend more than a certain amount on the Evening and the girls had made the sachets and needle-books out of scraps. Verity had a handsome patchwork pincushion and Margot received a blue china duck. Rosamund beamed over a home-made blotting pad with backs of cardboard covered with a remnant of cretonne and leaves of blotting-paper of every colour the school stationery cupboard could provide.

Miss O'Ryan had won the WEIGHT GUESSING and was awarded a pair of toy scales and weights; and Miss Denny, another mistress, triumphantly went up to take three packets of flower seeds for the SMELLING.

"And now, girls," when she had handed over the last prize and everyone was exclaiming, "Prayers! Clear the tables away and move the forms over. Catholics, go quietly to the Speisesaal. No more talking now, please."

Joan, who had contrived to enjoy herself reasonably well, despite her scorn of "baby games", was startled at the instant silence that fell. The Catholic girls lined up at the door and marched away while the rest folded the tables and put them into a corner, some of the Junior Middles running the long forms into their usual place across Hall. Meanwhile, Miss Lawrence, Head of the Music Staff, was at the piano, playing softly. Prefects handed out hymn books and then the Head came back, bearing the books she needed and Joan found that Prayers followed in a reverent atmosphere which was another shock to her. She resumed her air of scorn, and told herself that anything more idiotically "pi" she had never heard of. She stood stock still during the singing of the evening hymn, though Rosamund on one side of her and Alicia Leonard on the other both sang with all their hearts. When the girls knelt with folded hands and closed eyes, she was staring about her superciliously. As a result, when the Head had spoken the Blessing, and everyone rose from her knees, Joan was left kneeling, since she had not paid the slightest attention to what the Head was saying. She scrambled off them with a very red face and hastened to seat herself.

The Catholics arrived a minute later and they all repeated together the beautiful old Contakion: "Guard us waking; guard us sleeping; that waking, we may watch with Christ and sleeping, we may rest in Thee. Amen."

The elder girls, at any rate, were very fond of it, and despite herself, Joan was impressed by the sincerity with which they said it. She heard Rosamund's low voice repeating the beautiful old words devoutly and wondered. Just behind her came Verity Carey's silvery voice and she could see all the mistresses saying it with the Head. She had never bothered with prayers at home, merely casting off her clothes and tumbling into bed without even washing. When they finally got upstairs to Tulip, she found that not only were they expected to wash faces and hands and brush their hair thoroughly, but there came a sudden lull in the chatter and, when she addressed a remark to Carol Younger in the next cubicle, it remained unanswered. She looked through the curtain and saw that Carol was kneeling at her bedside, and when she peeped at Gwen Parry at the other side, the same thing was happening.

"Oh, lawks!" she thought. "Whatever is all this?"

She finished her undressing, patted her head perfunctorily with her brush and then got into bed—and this was where she found she was expected to wash, for Elinor Pennell's voice came from the far cubicle.

"Joan Baker! Has anyone showed you which bath cubicle you use?"

"No," Joan replied, sitting up. "Why?"

"I'll show you now." The curtains parted and Elinor stood there in her yellow dressing-gown. "Bring your things and come along. Anyone else not washed yet? Hurry up! The bell will go for Lights Out in five minutes!"

Two other girls scuttled off while Joan was pulling on her dressing-gown and bedroom slippers, and when she reached the bathroom with Elinor, sounds of vigorous splashing were to be heard. Elinor showed her where she was to go and retired to her own cubicle, and Joan, thinking all this was a stupid fuss, proceeded to wipe the powder and paint off her face and brush her teeth.

"You use this cubicle always," the prefect explained as they left the bathroom. "And I nearly forgot to tell you, but you must take your morning bath either cold or chill-off. Hot baths aren't allowed in the morning. You're second on the list after Elsie Morris. But I'll come along and tell you everything then. Now it's on the late side. The Lights Out bell will go in half a minute. Have you everything you want? Good-night, then. Sleep well."

Joan said good-night rather dazedly. It was news to her that she was expected to take a bath first thing in the morning. She wondered how Rosamund Lilley had met this and then remembered that Rosamund had told her that not even the boys went to bed without washing.

"Well, they say cleanliness is next to godliness," she thought as she lay down finally and pulled up the clothes, for the nights were still on the chilly side, May though it was. "At this rate I look like being forced to be both clean *and* godly! What a lot of silly fuss! I wonder if I'm going to like it here after all? Oh, well, if I find I can't stand it, Pa will take me away and send me somewhere else." Her jaw suddenly squared itself. "Oh no; that shan't happen! Ros Lilley's not going to have a single thing I don't have. I'll stick it somehow. But lawks, what a time I look like having!" After which, she turned over for the last time and fell asleep to dream that she had to take three baths a day and curtsy every time she spoke to a mistress until she fell over and woke up to find that she had fallen out of bed and Elinor was standing beside her asking if she had had a nightmare in very low tones before helping her to get up and remake her bed. After which she lay down again, and

69

when she dropped off she slept peacefully until the rising-bell woke her to another sunny morning.

CHAPTER VIII

JOAN TRIES IT ON

ROSAMUND'S difficulties began when she woke up next morning and remembered that she had been invited to spend the afternoon and evening at Freudesheim. In the shock of learning that Joan had arrived at the Chalet School she had forgotten it, but it came back when she opened her eyes to discover that it was a glorious day.

"What shall I do?" she thought to herself as she sat up to look out of the window. "The Head said I was to look after Joan for the first few days but I can't do it this afternoon if I'm out to tea. *Must* I go and tell Len I can't go? I don't want to—not for Joan Baker."

She sat forward, clasping her arms round her knees. It certainly was a problem and she could see no way to solve it at the moment. And yet, only a few weeks before, she would have been overjoyed to have Joan with her. What had come to her that last night she had felt not only did she not like her former friend, but felt ashamed of her—ashamed of the way she dressed and spoke and behaved.

"*Why* don't I like her now?" she pondered. "I was awfully fed up when Mum wouldn't let me go out with her. I used to think she was frightfully clever and daring and funny. Now, I don't feel I can bear her. Why?"

She could think of no answer—or not then. That the fortnight or so with girls who had other ideals and other standards than those of Joan Baker and her chums should already be making a difference to herself was beyond her. She just knew that where she had once admired, even though Joan had made her feel uncomfortable more than once, now she disliked her whole-heartedly.

The bell rang while she was trying to puzzle it out and she was first on the bath-list that morning, so she had to jump up, and go for her bath with the question still unanswered. But it worried her all the time she was bathing, dressing and tidying her cubicle. Even when she was ready in her pretty silk and wool frock of dusty pink, with her hair done in its long, smooth plaits, an immaculate handkerchief in her pocket and everything "just so" she was still worrying.

It stayed with her during Frühstück so that she had next to nothing to say, though the rest, taking full advantage of the fact that you might speak in any language you chose on Sunday, were chattering as hard as they could go. Joan had come downstairs made up and attired in another elaborate dress in vivid green this time. She wore bangles and a ring and her nails were varnished bright scarlet. As she looked round, she felt complacently that she was as smart as anyone and a good deal smarter than most. That Nemesis awaited her in the form of the House Matron was something that she had yet to learn. She looked scornfully at Rosamund's pretty frock and at the simple garments worn by the rest. Then she applied herself to the milky coffee, rolls and honey and fruit which formed the meal and felt scornful about that.

Mary-Lou Trelawney caught sight of Rosamund's troubled face and wondered. Being Mary-Lou, she could not let it alone, but when the girls were busy clearing the tables, made an opportunity to catch the younger girl and ask her what was wrong.

"You look as if you'd just heard that your entire family had been wiped out by an earthquake!" she said graphically. "What's up with you?"

"I don't know what to do," Rosamund said helplessly.

"What about? And hurry up and tell me! We've got to make our beds and *I've* got a letter to finish so there's no time to dither. What's happened?"

Mary-Lou's breezy manner had its effect on Rosamund. She began to feel a little less hopeless. She explained.

"You see, the Head said I was to look after the new girl, Joan Baker, for the first few days because I used to know her at home. But Mrs. Maynard has asked me to go to tea with the triplets this afternoon and if I do, how can I?"

Mary-Lou gave a moment to disentangling this confused statement. Then she said, "Nothing to worry about there that I can see. Someone else can look after Joan.

71

You aren't the only pebble on the beach, my good girl!"

She gave Rosamund a broad grin as she said it and Rosamund smiled back. "I didn't mean that. Only if the Head wants me to see to Joan——"

"Now you listen to me!" Mary-Lou interrupted her. "The Head meant that you were to see that she knows what to do and where to go; help her collect her books and stationery and all that sort of thing. She definitely didn't mean you to lose the chance of tea with Aunt Joey or she'd have said so at the time. She didn't, did she?"

"Oh, no. She simply said I was to look after her."

"Very well, then. That settles it. We'll fix up for someone to take Joan on while you're out. I can't do it myself. Verity and I are going up to the Rösleinalp straight from eleven o'clock service. Dad's coming for us in the car. But I'll think of someone else. You do what you can for Joan this morning and I'll fix her up with a partner for the afternoon ramble, and whoever it is can take her on till you get back. That'll be in time for Abendessen and you can take over again then. What form is she in?"

"I don't know, but I expect she'll be in Upper IVa, the same as me. We're the same age and we were in the same class at St. Matthew's."

Mary-Lou nodded and thought over the girls in that form. Then she nodded again. "I did think of Jo Scott, but I rather fancy she's off to Lucerne to see her people. They're living there just now, you know. But Betty Landon and Alicia Leonard are in that form and they're very decent about helping out when they're asked. I've just time to go and hunt them up. And you take that expression off your face and try to look a little more like a good Sunday! At present you look like Black Monday—and then some!" She chuckled infectiously and Rosamund, completely cheered up by this time, laughed with her.

"You're awfully decent! Thanks a lot!" she said fervently.

"Tosh! You'd do as much for me if I needed it. Better go and finish your home-letter. They have to be on the Slab before Mittagessen, you know."

With this parting piece of advice, she scudded off. Rosamund was developing great faith in the long-legged

Senior with the masterful manner, and she went off to her own letter, feeling completely happy.

As it was a fine day the girls were all out in the garden, and when Rosamund arrived she was greeted eagerly by Len who looked up from her own scribble.

"Come on, Rosamund! What an age you've been. I kept this chair for you; and I got this one for the new girl when she comes. Have you finished your letter?"

"Not quite," Rosamund said, opening her pad and extracting several sheets.

"What a lot you've done! I'm writing to Auntie Daisy and Con's writing to Auntie Rob. Auntie Daisy lives in Devonshire and Auntie Rob's a nun in Montreal. They were both at school here and they like to have all the news, so we two take it in turns to write. You'd love them if you knew them. They're ducks, both of them!"

Rosamund looked round. "I wonder if I ought to hunt Joan up? D'you know where she is?"

Margot Maynard came up with her boon companion, Emerence Hope, just then, and they both giggled.

"What's the joke?" Len demanded.

"Joan Baker!" Emerence said. "Matey—I mean our own Matey—came along ten minutes ago and she has her in our House Matron's room, asking why she's wearing any sort of make-up when she isn't sixteen yet!"

"How d'you know?" Con inquired, looking up from her letter. "Oh, and have you any message for Auntie Rob, Margot? You'd better take this sheet and send her something or she'll be talking."

"We know," Emerence said, "because I'm in Tulip this term and we were all there when Matey barged in and demanded her. She said, 'Is Joan Baker here? Come with me to Matron's room. I want a little talk with you about make-up.' So we all knew what was coming next."

"I did try to say something to her about it not being allowed for anyone but Seniors, when we were at break—I mean Frühstück—but she wouldn't listen. She's used make-up for years now—out of school."

"But this isn't out of school," observed Con, looking up from her letter. "It never is in term time. And anyhow, no one's going to let her go round looking like that. I

73

heard Vi Lucy saying you could scrape the stuff off with a knife! Mamma's told us often that when the time comes if we *want* to use it, we can, but it's got to be properly."

Margot, who had accepted her sister's offer and was scribbling away at a note to her nun aunt, looked up and laughed. "I don't suppose I'll bother with it till I'm grown up. It takes me all my time to be down on time in the mornings as it is. If I had to spend ages powdering my nose and sticking my lips I'd never do it."

"I think it's all rot," said Emerence, who might be fifteen in years but was considerably younger in everything else. "And a fearful waste of money."

"But that's how Joan *likes* to spend her money," Rosamund sighed, looking worried.

"Matey'll tell her where she gets off," Emerence said with a grin. "Don't you worry about it, Rosamund. But what asses her people must be," she added wonderingly. "My folk let me do pretty much what I like, but I can just hear them if I'd started to paint my face even now!"

This, from a girl who had been brought up on the principle that you should never say "no" to a child, carried more weight with the triplets than Rosamund who had no idea of Emerence's earlier history. However, she felt that the latter young person was quite right in saying that Matron would deal with the matter. There had never yet been a girl, not even Emerence herself, who had dared to stand up to Matron for long. Rosamund didn't think Joan Baker was likely to prove the exception to the rule. She turned her attention to reading through her letter before adding the final paragraph. That done, she settled down to writing and had just finished and was folding the sheets for the envelope when Joan arrived.

Joan looked like a thundercloud. Matron had dealt well and truly with her and the first attempt at defiance on the new girl's part had brought her such a rebuke that she had been instantly silent. She had been sent to wash her face and remove the scarlet varnish from her nails. Then Matron had examined her dresses and picked out the only schoolgirl frock of the lot and bade her change.

So subdued was Joan, that she had done as she was told without remark. But inwardly she was raging. Matron had sent her out to the garden till church time and she had come to seek Rosamund and let fly about everything.

Rosamund saw her coming and jumped up. "Come along, Joan," she said, speaking as cordially as she could. "Here's a chair for you. Have you done your home letter yet? Oh, but you'd send the postcard, of course, to let your people know you've arrived safely."

"I've sent it," Joan said furiously, "and if I'd known what this place was like, I wouldn't be here to send it, I can tell you. I'm going to tell Pa and Ma *all* about it when I *do* write, I can tell you! Interfering with the way I'm dressed! I'll bet my frocks cost a lot more than anything that old Frozen Limit ever spent on her clothes! They came from one of the biggest shops in Brighton, but because they don't happen to suit *her* taste they're all to be packed up except this thing and sent back, and Ma's to be asked for leave to buy me two here that are 'more fitting'. What's wrong with them, I'd like to know? And who's she to say what I can or can't wear?"

The triplets and Emerence had listened to her in wide-eyed silence. Rosamund was not so surprised. She knew Joan. She tried to smooth things over.

"You see, Joan, at school you are supposed to wear plain sort of frocks. We all do, even the prefects and the big girls at St. Mildred's House. You don't want not to be like everyone else, do you? You can wear those other dresses in the hols. And that blue's awfully pretty."

"You *would*!" Joan spoke with the utmost scorn in her voice. "Grandpa chose it. Ma and I picked the others and it's a mean shame to send them back. I'd never have come to a hole like this if I'd known they were so fussy."

The others had listened in silence and something in the atmosphere of the little group had kept Joan from the worst excesses in language. But her final remark was too much for Emerence.

"The Chalet School is *not* a hole," she said, almost as furiously as Joan had spoken. "It's a jolly fine school and you're jolly lucky to be here, let me tell you!"

She stopped there, for Len had kicked her quietly. No one wanted a fuss. That might mean having a mistress or a prefect in charge of them during their free time and the school at large was proud of the fact that they were, to a very great extent, left to themselves out of lessons. Emerence guessed what she meant and fell silent.

Joan, not understanding these wheels within wheels, laughed raucously. "Yes; you'd better hold your tongue!" she said with a sneer. "*And* don't address your elders and betters so rudely, neither."

Margot smiled sweetly. "Oh, but if you come to that, Emerence *is* your elder."

"I don't believe it!" Joan retorted with a look at the childish-looking Emerence.

"How old——" began Con, but Rosamund interfered.

"Emerence is a year older than you are, Joan. She had her fifteenth birthday last week. We had a gorgeous cake at our table for it," she added reminiscently.

Thus proved wrong, Joan was again silenced. She felt unsure of herself among these girls and she was furious to see that Rosamund Lilley fitted in among them to the manner born. She let the subject drop, took the chair kept for her and turned to stare sulkily across the lawn while the others, thankful that there had been no real trouble, returned to their letters.

Joan continued to have nothing to say when they were called to put on their hats for church. She knew that this was an invariable part of boarding-school life and accepted it. But when they were walking back after the short bright service, Rosamund seized the opportunity to tell her that as she herself was going out for the afternoon and evening, Betty and Alicia would look after her.

"I'm sorry, Joan," she began, "but I shan't be with you this afternoon."

Joan turned and stared at her. "Oh? Why not?"

"Well, you see I'm going home with the Maynards," Rosamund explained. "I was asked before we knew it was you coming. They live next door, you know."

"I *don't* know! And I think it's downright mean of you to go off to a party and leave me alone my first day here!"

"I'm sorry about that," Rosamund acknowledged, "and I did wonder if I ought to ask Mrs. Maynard to excuse me; but the Head sent for me before we went to church

76

and said it would be all right for me to go. Alicia Leonard and Betty Landon are going to look after you and you have a ramble this afternoon and then church again after Kaffee und Kuchen, so you'll be all right."

"Why can't I come with you?" Joan demanded.

"Oh, I couldn't do that! I only just know Mrs. Maynard. Did you know that she's Josephine M. Bettany that writes all those gorgeous books—*Cecily Holds the Fort* and *Werner of the Alps* and *Tessa Takes the Trail* and all the rest? I'm simply thrilled to be going to tea with her!" Rosamund added happily.

"I don't believe you!" Joan retorted.

"Oh, but it's true. She was at the Chalet School and Mary-Lou Trelawney says that in one way she's never really left. Anyhow, she asked me to go with the triplets this afternoon and I'm going. We were to have gone before, but they have a new baby, so Mrs. Maynard had to put us off till today. I've seen Cecil. She's a lovely baby! "

"Well, why don't you ask those three kids if I can come? They ought to be glad to have me—just come from England. You're jolly pally with them, I notice. Ask them! "

Rosamund shook her head. "I couldn't possibly—not the very first time I'm asked there myself."

"Then if you won't, *I* will!"

"Joan! You can't! You hardly know them! You can't go asking them for invites!"

"Can't I just! I'll tell you what it is, Ros Lilley, you're getting more than a bit above yourself and you'd better mind yourself or I'll see that the rest know *all* about you."

Rosamund stared at her. "What *are* you getting at? There's nothing to tell."

"Oh, isn't there? Think your precious Mrs. Maynard would be so keen to have you and her triplets so pally if she knew your mother was just someone's servant before her marriage and your Pa was just a common market gardener? Or that you're here through Mrs. Gay's charity? For that's all you are—a charity schoolgirl! "

Rosamund flushed at the taunt but before she could reply, Vi Lucy, a member of Va and one of Mary-Lou's great friends, came running up to say that as the service

77

had been shorter than usual, they might stroll on a little instead of going straight back to school, only now they must line up as it meant walking along the great motor-coach road.

The school always went to church in line, but on coming out were allowed to break up into pairs and groups so long as they behaved properly. Hence the possibility of Joan's remarks to Rosamund, for the pair of them had been walking a little apart from the others.

"Wait here," Vi said. "You two are much too far ahead. *You* ought to know, Rosamund, even if Joan doesn't, that we aren't allowed to go racing off like that."

"I'm sorry," Rosamund said meekly. "We—we were—talking and I never noticed."

Vi noticed her hesitation at once but said nothing about it. She merely warned them to keep with the rest another time and then went on to catch up with a bunch of Vb people who had transgressed even more than Rosamund and Joan had done. But later on she remembered it and mentioned it to Mary-Lou when the pair were discussing the day's happenings. Mary-Lou shook her head and observed that she didn't particularly care for what she had seen of Joan Baker. There it was left for the present; but both Mary-Lou and Vi remembered it later on.

Meanwhile, Joan was enjoying the sense of triumph her final remarks to Rosamund had given her. She had little fear that the other girl would refuse to knuckle under to her with a threat like that held over her. She said no more just then. The others coming up made it wiser to hold her tongue.

As for Rosamund, she was not really disturbed by Joan's very unpleasant epithet. She had the sense to know that her scholarship was by no means a form of charity. But she *was* worried about Joan's remarks about her mother and father. Three weeks in the school had already changed her outlook considerably, but she still remembered some of the very silly cheap stories she had read and she wondered whether the Chalet School girls, friendly as they were, would care to have much to do with her if they knew her history. Joan had always held it over her that while Mrs. Lilley had been a housemaid, Mrs. Baker had been a "young lady" in a shop. It had been well for Rosamund that Charmian had chanced to overhear some remarks like this once, and when she had her young sister alone, had seen to it that she understood that it was a lot of silly nonsense and their mother was much more ladylike. But Charmian was not here to guard her sister and Rosamund worried for the rest of the walk.

Joan seized her chance when they met alone in the common room a minute or two before Mittagessen. Rosamund had gone to put her library-book away in the cupboard and Joan, lounging down the corridor, had seen her and followed. No one else was there and Joan's eyes lit up with malicious glee. She had her chance.

"You mind what I said to you, Ros Lilley," she said, standing between the cupboard door and the room so that Rosamund was pushed into a corner. "You get me an invite from Mrs. Maynard for some day soon or I shan't half have something to tell the rest! I've warned you."

Rosamund said nothing. She merely watched her chance and slid round Joan and out of the room, leaving that young woman to consider how best she could carry out her threat if her orders were not obeyed.

CHAPTER IX

JOEY TO THE RESCUE!

"WELL, here you all are! Come along! We're in the garden this afternoon. And don't yell more than you must. Cecil is asleep and I want her to remain so! "

Thus Joey Maynard, when her triplets and Rosamund appeared through the gates in the hedge that separated the Chalet School grounds from those of Freudesheim. She kissed her own girls and then held out her hands and drew Rosamund into the circle. "Don't stand back there looking as if you didn't belong and didn't want to! Freudesheim is part of the school as I hope you find out very quickly. I'm delighted to see you, Rosamund, and I hope you'll find your way over here quite often. Any chums of our girls are always welcome."

Rosamund found herself giving smile for smile. She liked this friendly person enormously already. She liked her lovely voice, her eyes like black pansies, the way her black hair lay in a straight fringe across her broad brows and was plaited into great flat earphones over her ears. Above all, she liked her friendliness. It was so clearly real.

"I couldn't be shy with her, ever," the new girl thought as she replied as prettily as she could to Joey's welcome.

Joey herself liked what she saw in Rosamund, but she noted a faintly worried look in the deep grey eyes and she wondered what had caused it. "I must get to the bottom of this," she thought as she tucked one hand in Rosamund's arm, the other through Len's and, followed by Con and Margot, marched them all round the side of the house to the pleasant lawn where a slight dark girl was sitting on a groundsheet with two small very fair people, helping them to build a brick house. A bigger boy was busy with some pieces of string and the big pram stood to one side with the light carefully shaded from its tiny occupant.

Joey called, "Maria, meet my big girls!" And she turned to look and then sprang to her feet, dark eyes wide with amazement as she stared at the triplets.

"Joey Bettany—I mean Maynard—are you telling me that these leggy objects are the chubby babies we all used to scrap over cuddling? It's impossible! "

She had almost as charming a voice as Mrs. Maynard, with a very slight accent. She was darker even than Joey, and in repose her face was sad. Now it was lit up with laughter as she regarded the embarrassed triplets.

"My three eldest," Joey said nonchalantly. "I told you you'd get a shock when you saw them. They're quite elderly people now—wicked Middles, no less! "

"No wickeder than you used to be—they couldn't! " Maria retorted. "Which is which? Oh, but you said Len was the tallest of the lot, so this must be Len. I see she's still got the red hair though it's much darker."

"Oh, my dear, I got the shock of my life when I found that they weren't all going to *stay* red!" Joey assured her with a peal of laughter. "This is Con, and Margot, as you see, is red-gold. It really has been just as well. If they'd remained as alike as they were when they were babies, I can see them having us all running up the walls!"

Maria laughed. The triplets looked at each other with deep regret.

"What a pity!" Len said. "If only we'd all stayed alike we *could* have had some fun!"

"Couldn't we just!" Margot remarked with fervour.

Con's brown eyes danced wickedly. "Just think of it!" she said. "We could have swopped over all sorts of things and no one would have known. It's hard luck!"

Joey stopped laughed. "Don't you worry, my lambs," she said severely. "*I* should have known t'other from which, I assure you! I never muddled you when you were babies. I'm not likely to do it at this late stage, even if you'd remained completely identical. Well, it's only the two eldest boys you haven't seen now, Maria"—Rosamund noted that she pronounced it the continental way, "Mareea", and liked it—"and if you've seen Jack, you've seen Steve. He's Papa's image. Charles is a complete hop-out-o'-kin. He has my black hair, but that's all. And now, this fourth girl is Rosamund Lilley, new this term. Rosamund, this is Fräulein Marani who used to be at the school in the Dark Ages. And," she added with some indignation, "I like her cheek accusing me of wickedness! She wasn't any angel herself!" She grinned fiendishly at Maria, "you never tried to poke your head through the back of a chair, did you—and have to have the said back sawn in half to release you?"[1]

"*Joey!*" Maria cried, going crimson.

"And," went on Joey relentlessly, "who was it that painted her face to play Red Indians at Oberammergau when we went there for the Passion Play, and had to be marched back to the Gasthaus down the village street, looking like something out of the nearest looney-bin?"[1]

"You're a *mean*, Joey Bettany!" cried Maria. Then she began to laugh. "Do you mean to tell me that you've treasured up all those memories till now?"

"Oh, not me only," Joey said airily. "It's all down in

[1] The Chalet School and Jo.

the unwritten annals of the school. You and your crowd of little angels made history on those occasions."

Maria threw up her hands in horror. "How terrible! There's only one consolation," she added, "and that is that your own exploits were far more and much worse."

"Granted. But I've never tried to turn a blind eye to them," retorted Joey. "Hi, Mike! Where are you off to? Come and say hello to Rosamund and then you and the babies are going out with Maria."

Mike, who had been trying to sneak off unobserved, came back reluctantly and held out an unclean paw. "How d'ye do? Very well thank you!" he gabbled, hurriedly pulling his fingers away as Rosamund touched them.

"Your manners!" his mother said resignedly. "Go and wash and be ready for Maria when she calls. Go with him, Con, and see that he doesn't swim the bathroom out." Then she turned to her visitor. "The fact of the matter is," she said as Mike fled, pursued by his second sister, "he's got to the stage where he has no use for kissing. People always seem to want to do it—the result of his cherubic face and curls—and he loathes it. He's a boy, thank goodness! Soon Felix will be copying him. This is Felix; and here's his twin, Felicity."

The milk-fair twins held up their faces at once to be kissed. They were like Mike in having their mother's delicate, mobile features, but their flaxen curls and general fairness made them a great contrast to even Margot. Rosamund knelt to give the kisses and Felicity promptly begged her to come and see the castle they were building.

"Later," Fräulein Marani said, taking a hand of each. "Now, we're going for a walk. Come along and put on your hats. I'll come back for Cecil when they're ready, Joey."

"Very well," Joey replied. She turned to look at the pram over which Len and Margot were bending. "Mind you don't wake her up. Maria won't want to trundle her around the Platz yelling her head off. Len, go and look in the top right-hand drawer of my desk and you'll find a box of sweets. Margot, run to the kitchen and tell Anna it's time she went. I can manage perfectly well now."

As the pair obeyed her, she turned to Rosamund laughing. "Anna has been with me ever since my marriage and she seems to think that I can't spare her. She has made quite a number of friends since we came here and could go out nearly every day, but I have to insist or she'd simply stick around. Here's a comfy chair. Sit down and tell me how you like school so far."

"Lots better than I expected," Rosamund replied.

Joey glanced at her quickly. "Didn't you want to come? Tell me later," she added as Len arrived bearing a large box. "We'll have a private chat."

"Oh, Mamma, you are a pet!" Len exclaimed as she deposited the box in her mother's lap. "Our very favourite collection!"

"Oh, we had to celebrate Rosamund's first visit here," Joey said, opening it. "Have one, Rosamund. I can recommend those green affairs."

"The sugared nuts are gorgeous," Len remarked.

Rosamund laughed and took a green sweet. "They all look smash—er—marvellous! Thank you, Mrs. Maynard."

Maria came to collect the pram and Joey accompanied the party to the gate and waved them off while a stout pleasant-looking woman appeared, spoke to her mistress and then also departed, by which time Margot had joined the party on the lawn, bringing Con with her.

Joey sat down again, handed her sweets round and then said, "And now, tell me all the hanes! Is Mary-Lou as well as ever? How is Auntie Doris?"

The triplets tumbled over themselves to reply and, for the next hour or so, Rosamund was frequently left breathless at the knowledge of the school that Joey betrayed. She made eager inquiries about at least a dozen people. The triplets, in their turn, had any number of questions to ask about people they knew.

"How's Nina's cousin, Mamma?" Len demanded after a little talk about Nina Rutherford.

"Just a shade a better this week, thank goodness! Papa says if she goes on improving it won't be long before she can have visitors. She's out on the verandah you know, and people could go and stand below and talk to her. But not yet. She's much too weak for any excitement."

"It's Nina Rutherford's cousin, Alix Rutherford," Len

explained to her friend. "She's been awfully ill and they sent her to the San up here. That was last term, and she's never been able to see anyone but her father and mother, so far. When she's really better, though, some of the Sixth and St. Mildred's are going to visit her. She's more their age. And Nina will go, too, of course."

Rosamund knew Nina Rutherford and had sat gasping to hear when she had played to them one evening. It seemed amazing to her that any girl just a year or so older than herself could play like that.

"What's wrong with her?" she asked.

"She had pneumonia and pleurisy and it left lung trouble," Joey said swiftly.

"Does Papa think she'll get all right?" Con asked as she surveyed the tempting rows of sweets. "I'll have this cherry, I think. What did he say about it, Mamma?"

"Too soon to be definite, my lamb. They all hope so. Try one of those violets, Rosamund."

"Mother, Emmy had a letter yesterday and her people are coming next term to spend Christmas here for the winter sports," Margot said, changing the subject.

"Are they really? She'll be thrilled! Where are they staying? Not up here, I suppose?"

"No; at Grindelwald. Emmy was wondering if you'd let us go for a week or so in the hols to stay with them."

"Too soon to say yet. It would depend on quite a lot of things. Ask me nearer the time. You know Emerence, don't you, Rosamund? Aren't you in the same form?"

"Yes; she sits on one side of me," Rosamund said shyly.

"She came tenth in the form list last week," remarked Len with a full mouth.

"You'll choke if you try to talk like that," her mother said detachedly. "What about you people?"

"Con was seventh, bracketed with Sue Meadows, and I was top with Alicia," Len replied having got rid of her mouthful. "And you were fourteenth, weren't you, Rosamund? It's jolly good you know, seeing you've never done any French or German till you came here. She beat seven other people, Mamma."

Joey smiled at Rosamund. "I think it's excellent. How

are you managing about the languages, by the way? I hope you don't find it *too* hard."

"Oh, it was awful at first!" Rosamund said fervently. "I couldn't understand a thing that was said to me and I couldn't reply when I *did* understand. It's a wee bit easier now because I do know things like 'yes' and 'no' and 'I don't understand' and things like that. And Mdlle's been awfully decent. She gives me ten new words to learn every day and hears me any time she meets me and helps me to say them right. And Len and Con help, too. I really do know a lot more than I did."

Joey laughed. "I can sympathise. Oh, not French or German. From the time I was a little older than Mike, we spent all our holidays abroad and I picked up any amount of both. But the year I left school, I went to India to spend six months with my brother who was in the forestry there, and I'll never forget the awful feeling of helplessness when I heard Hindustani all round me and couldn't understand a word! I soon picked it up, of course, but just at first it felt dreadful!"

"Have you really been to India?" Rosamund exclaimed.

"Have I not! *And* Canada, as I expect the girls have told you. One day we're all going back for another visit. Oh, not yet!" as the triplets looked up eagerly. "We've got to save up our pennies for a trip like that."

"And see Auntie Rob," Len finished joyfully. "I'll tell Cordélie the next time I write. She'll be thrilled! She asked in her letter last if there was any chance of our crossing before we were both finished with school. When will it be, do you think?—Next summer hols?"

"My dear girl, I can't possibly say at the moment. I'll want Cecil trotting about anyhow. I don't fancy having a baby in arms *and* the twins *and* Mike to look after all at once. Yes; I know you three would help. Perhaps when you three are Seniors. But Auntie Rob's in Montreal, you know, and Cordélie and the rest of your Canadian friends are in Toronto."

"I know, but if we went at all, we wouldn't miss Montreal," Len said shrewdly. "And we'll be thirteen in November and that's only two years off being a Senior. O.K., I'll tell Cordélie she'll have to wait at least two years. And you can let Marie-Adelaïde know, too, Con."

Margot tossed her golden head. "Well, I haven't written to Amélie for ages now *or* heard from her, so I shan't bother. The other two can tell her."

Joey looked at her daughter but said nothing. Instead she suggested that the triplets should go and see about tea while she took Rosamund round the garden.

"Anna's left everything ready," she said. "Light the stove under the kettle, Len, and bring the things out. Don't go to the Saal, though. Papa's asleep there and I don't want him disturbed until tea's ready. He was late last night and he had to go off early this morning."

The triplets went off and Joey caught Rosamund's hands and pulled her to her feet. "Come along, Rosamund, I want to show off our rose garden. Len told me your father was a gardener, so I expect you're keen, too."

"Oh, I am!" Rosamund said. "If I didn't want to be an air hostess I'd have gone in for gardening, I think. But I'd love to travel about and see the world, so I thought I'd have a shot at it—either that or lady courier."

"A very good idea," Joey agreed, opening a little gate. "Now, Rosamund, what about this?"

Rosamund looked round and her eyes lit up. "Oh! How simply sma—I mean wizard!"

"You mayn't believe it, but when we came here, this was a cabbage patch. We dug them up and had it properly turfed with beds for the roses. Now it's as you see it. And all our own doing. Gaudenz from the school dug it up for us and helped us to put down the turf. The rest, we've done. You know," she spoke with a chuckle, "I'd like your father to see it and say what he thought."

"Dad would be thrilled," Rosamund said. "Of course, nowadays, he mostly works in the glasshouses; but he began at the bottom and he knows all about what you have to do to get a result like this. He works for Sheldon and Bosbury. They go in for a lot for roses, too."

It had come out quite naturally. She had no idea, of course, that Joey already knew most of what there was to know from Tom Gay. Neither did she know that this bringing her to the rose garden had been in the nature of a test. Joey Maynard had never had the slightest use for snobs and she wanted to see if the girl would talk openly about her people.

But Rosamund had made up her mind. The talk she had just heard had told her that Mrs. Maynard contrived to keep a finger on the school's pulse and she felt that that lady would soon tell her how the girls would feel if they knew that her mother had been a housemaid and her father was a working gardener. It came bubbling out. Rosamund said not a word about Joan Baker and her threats; but what she did say told Joey that there was something in the background and she proceeded to disabuse the girl's mind with her usual vigour.

"My dear girl, when you've been at the Chalet School a little longer, you won't worry in the least about it. The school has always been taught that what matters is the girl herself—is she decent and sporting? Does she pull her weight? *That's* what matters here. And so far as that goes, my lamb, we all of us are the descendants of a gardener. Have you forgotten that when God created Adam, He put him into Eden with orders to look after it? And who do you imagine did the housework but Eve? She hadn't any servants that I've ever heard of! And for goodness' sake *don't* go judging this school by the silly ones you read about in the fourpenny weeklies! And another thing, Rosamund. When God chose a Mother for His Son, He didn't choose a queen or even a great lady, but a village girl who was engaged to the village carpenter. And our Blessed Lord's friends were all working men— unless Judas wasn't. But that didn't hinder them from being gentlemen or Our Lady from being the greatest Lady in the world. After that, how *could* any human being put on airs and be unkind to other people because they came from working-class families. Oh, no! You need never be afraid of that sort of thing here."

"I never thought of it like that," Rosamund said.

"Well, don't forget for the future. And remember this as well. It's a pleasant thing to know that one comes from a long line of gentle folk," Joey used the words separately, "but it only means you've a lot to live up to. But when you come to the root of matters, it's you—*you*—You that matters all the time—what *you* are! Now do you see?"

Rosamund nodded. "Yes, I think so. And—and you won't want Len and Con to stop being friends with me?"

"Talk sense! The only thing that would make me try to stop the friendship would be if you turned out a rotter and a snob! I hope you and my girls will go on being chums. I *want* them to have friends apart from each other. *You* want friends apart from your family. That's right and natural. You'll meet all sorts as you go through the world, and let me tell you you've as much right to hold up your head and be proud of your people, who have tried to put decent things and good things into you, as anyone! Go ahead, all of you, and be as chummy as you like! I'm glad of it! And don't mind if anyone else says things. In *this* school you aren't very likely to meet it, I'm thankful to say. Anyone who comes here feeling that way very soon gets the nonsense knocked out of her. Oh, and take that worried look off your face! It doesn't," Joey concluded with a gurgle of laughter, "suit your type of beauty. Now let's go and see if tea's ready!"

She took Rosamund back to the side lawn where Dr. Maynard was patiently waiting for his tea and Maria had returned with the small fry. After tea, which was a riotous affair, Cecil had to be attended to and then she was handed round for everyone to cuddle. Mercifully, she was a placid baby and took quite kindly to being passed about. Her bedtime came next and Joey took Len and Rosamund up to the night nursery to help, sending the other two to clear away and talk to their father.

Maria attended to the twins and Mike, and when the babies were all safely in bed, Rosamund was shown all over the house, including the study where she regarded the long line of gaily jacketed books to which Joey laid claim as hers with awe. It changed to delight when the gifted authoress rooted in a cupboard and produced a copy of her first book which she presented to her visitor.

All in all, it was a delightful tea-party and the four finally returned to school in high glee which only changed to dismay when Len stopped dead in the gateway to exclaim, "Oh! Mamma hasn't told us why Mary-Lou's so important and she said she would!"

"There isn't time now," Margot replied. "You stop

nattering and come on or the Abbess will think twice about letting us go again this term! We've two minutes before Abendessen! Scram!"

It was quite enough. They "scrammed" in short order.

CHAPTER X

CHECK FOR JOAN

JOAN'S real difficulties began next day when, to her horror, she discovered that not only were all lessons taken in French, the official language for the day, but that, from the moment she got up to the moment of lights out, she was expected to do her best to speak and understand the language herself. Since she did not know a word she had to be helped continually. Everyone was extremely patient with her. But she was too much taken up with grumbling to herself to realize this. Especially was she resentful of the fact that Rosamund, who had come to school equally ignorant, had tried her hardest and was able to understand a little and even to speak a little. It must be owned that Rosamund's French was all too often helped out with plain English or a queer polyglot affair that was neither English nor French. But, shy girl as she was, she stuck to it and was making real progress.

Now Joan's real motive for insisting on coming to the Chalet School had been one of jealousy. She had been furious when she heard that Canon and Mrs. Gay had chosen Rosamund to hold their scholarship. She had never bothered much with her lessons at St. Matthew's, but she considered that she was miles ahead of "that silly, babyish kid, Ros Lilley", and for the said "kid" to have stepped above her in such a way roused all her worst feelings. When her father, backed up by her grandfather, insisted that she and Pamela must go to a good school for at least two more years, it had struck her that it would be quite pleasant to go as a paying pupil to the same school.

She had laid her plans. She would tighten her grip on Rosamund—she had quite sufficient brains to know that she had had a big influence on that young woman—and also patronise her; and that would be quite pleasant, too. She had seen the prospectus Miss Dene had sent her grandfather when he first wrote and had learned from it that foreign languages were spoken on certain days of the week, but she had not really grasped all that it implied. On this Monday morning realisation broke over her in full flood.

It began when the rising-bell went and Elinor Pennell made the rounds to be certain that every girl was up and beginning on the duties of the day. She duly came to Joan's cubicle to warn her to be ready to follow Gwen Parry to the bathroom and found her still snoozing comfortably in bed.

"Joan! Eveillez-vous!" she said authoritatively. "Vous vous baignez quand Gwen Parry est retournée. Dèpêchez-vous de vous lever, s'il vous plaît! "

Joan sat up. "I was ever so comfy," she grumbled.

"En français, s'il vous plaît," Elinor said. "Levez-vous! "

"Eh?" asked Joan.

Elinor patiently repeated her remarks, speaking still more slowly. Joan grasped Gwen's name and guessed that "retournée" meant "returned", so she said, "What about Gwen? *I* don't know where she is. Returned from where?"

Seeing that she really did not know even this elementary French, Elinor repeated her words in English and then in French, concluding with, "Et maintenant, le répétez, s'il vous plaît—repeat what I've said, Joan. It will help you to learn the language."

"Oh, raspberries to that!" Joan said rudely. "You don't expect me to talk French all the time, do you? If you do, you've another guess coming."

Those of the Middles who heard her, gasped, and Elinor bit her lip. She had Francie Wilford and Heather Clayton in Tulip and they were two demons at any time. It was fortunate for her that Heather was in the bathroom and Francie, far from wanting to copy this very impudent new girl, felt indignant that anyone should cheek one of *their* prefects in this way and gave tongue on the subject later.

A sharp reproof was on Elinor's tongue, but she controlled herself and said quietly, speaking in English that there might be no mistake, "Oh yes, Joan. Here, we speak nothing but French on Mondays and Thursdays. Tuesdays and Fridays, it's German. We have English on Wednesdays, Saturdays, and Sundays, too, for all English girls. Don't be afraid," she added with a smile. "It really isn't as hard as it sounds. Everyone will try to help you and if you hear nothing but French all round you, you can't help picking up a certain amount. Keep on trying and you'll soon find you're beginning to understand quite a good deal. Now, will you please get up—'levez-vous' means 'get up' —because it's your turn for the bath next."

Joan scrambled out of bed with a very ill grace. "I had a bath yesterday morning and I washed my face and hands last night. I'm clean enough. It's a lot of footling rot, all this washing and bathing."

Elinor eyed her with distinct astonishment, though all she said was, "It's a rule of the school. Be quick— Dépêchez-vous! Gwen s'est retournée, et Elsie Morris se baigne la prochaine!" She gave Joan her dressing-gown.

Joan put it on, shuffled her feet into her slippers and then marched off to the bathroom, looking very black. Gwen had left the tap running for her. Joan turned it off, made a face at it and—deliberately ignored it. She washed her face and hands and cleaned her teeth and departed for Tulip dormitory where Elsie Morris was impatiently awaiting her turn. As soon as Joan arrived she shot off and Miss Joan went to her cubicle feeling better. At least she had "done" the authorities over the bath!

She dressed and, warned by what had happened the day before, had the sense to let her face alone. She had no desire for a second interview with "Matey", as the girls all affectionately called Matron Gould who was the doyenne of the domestic staff. Finally, she emerged from her cubicle looking like an ordinary schoolgirl in her school frock of soft blue cotton. As it was a uniform dress, there was no chance of touching it up and she looked really nice, if she could have seen it. As it was, she stared at her reflection in the mirror and grumbled to herself, "Of all the dowdy deadly dull things! Oh, well, I guess I'll just have to stick it for this term, anyhow. I doubt if I'll last longer."

She had stripped her bed after a fashion. She folded

her pyjamas, tumbled her brush and comb into her bureau locker and came out of her cubicle feeling complacently that she had done everything that was required of her. She was due for another shock, however, for Elinor, coming from her own domain, asked her softly, "Have you said your prayers?"

Joan stared at her. Then she looked round and was suddenly struck by the silence round her. "Do you mean we're supposed to say prayers on our own?" she gasped.

"Certainly," Elinor said. "Go back and say yours."

Joan went back and remained for about two minutes, gabbling over Our Father. Then she got up and came out again to find most of the others out and tossing up their curtains over the standards to let the fresh air from the windows sweep unhindered through the room. Joan watched them, open-mouthed. Gwen saw and came to her.

"Il faut lever vos rideaux," she said; and suited the action to the word by flinging Joan's curtains up, thus exposing that young woman's idea of stripping a bed.

There was no time to talk. Gwen acted. She pulled the bedclothes off the bed and threw them over the chair, shaking up the pillow and laying it on top of the bureau locker. Then she turned the mattress, leaving it humped up so that the air could pass under it.

Joan watched her with dropping jaw. "What on earth——?" she gasped.

Gwen turned to say, "En français, s'il vous plaît!"

Joan was so stunned, that she had nothing to say. She meekly followed Gwen down the room to join the line of girls waiting at the door until the bell should ring and they might go downstairs. Her own idea of bed-making was to tumble out in the morning, shake up her pillow, pull the clothes straight and see that at least the bed *looked* tidy. This drastic treatment was quite new to her.

Elinor, very fresh and dainty in her uniform frock of soft pink, came to straighten the line and, when the bell rang, to march them out of the room on the tail of Wallflower which came before Tulip, and see them downstairs. Once they were there, she went off to the prefects' room while the younger girls went to the House common room.

It came as another shock to Joan to find when they got there that though no one in authority was with them the rest still spoke French. It is true that some of the accents and literal translations from English were enough to make any Frenchman tear his hair in horror, but it was French of a sort. If anyone was stuck, she applied to someone who might be able to help her and repeated what she was given. What was more, when she herself spoke to anyone else in English, she was instantly told the French for her remark and expected to repeat it. Before they were summoned to Frühstück, she had already learned two phrases —"En français, s'il vous plaît" and "Répétez celà!"

After Frühstück and Prayers—during which latter Joan was appalled to note that French was still spoken—they went upstairs to make their beds and dust their cubicles.

"Lot of nonsense!" Joan growled to herself as she set to work to flatten the mattress and then toss sheets and blanket on without much tucking in. Matron of St. Agnes, the House where she was domiciled, arrived to show her the only way of bedmaking approved at the school before she had done more than settle undersheet and blanket and she was shown the art with great firmness and in fluent French. She was not to know that Matron Henschell was, herself, an Old Girl of the Chalet School. She was quite young—but Barbara Henschell had been a most competent prefect during the last two years of her school life, and Joan found that the bed must be properly made and her little domain in speckless order before she was released and put on her hat for the early walk. The sun was gaining power now and the road along which the school took their morning walks was unshaded and no one wanted any cases of sun or heat stroke to cope with.

Rosamund met her on the path outside the main building where Upper IVa, to which form Joan had been assigned for the moment, were congregating. She was in Ste. Thérèse's, the school house, and as St. Agnes' was at the far end of the buildings, they had only seen each other at Frühstück and then were too far apart to talk.

"Bon jour, Joan," she said with a sturdy British accent. "Voulez-vous—er—marchez avec moi?"

"Voulez-vous vous promenez," remarked Maeve Bettany

who was passing and heard this. "Se promener—to go for a walk, et ne l'oubliez pas," she added with a grin.

"Merci beaucoup," Rosamund said. "Je me le rapellerez à l'avenir."

Maeve grinned again and went to join up with Sue Meadows and Joan gaped at Rosamund amazedly. "And where did *you* learn French?" she demanded.

Her high-pitched voice rose above the subdued chatter of the others and attracted the attention of Miss O'Ryan who had just come on escort duty with them.

"Qui est-ce qui parle en anglais?" she demanded sharply. "Payez une amende, s'il vous plaît!"

Rosamund took a step towards her, "S'il vous plaît, Joan ne sait pas de français," she stammered.

Biddy O'Ryan nodded. "Merci, Rosamund. Maintenant, je comprends, et l'amende est remis. Rosamund, aide Joan toujours, je vous en prie."

"Oui, Mademoiselle," Rosamund said reddening again, for Joan's eyes looked as if they would drop out.

Miss O'Ryan smiled and nodded and then called the girls to order and set them marching off down the drive and out into the one made road the Görnetz Platz boasted. It led from the coachroad through the mountains right to the end where the great new Sanatorium stood. Towards the mountain flanks there were pines, but here the grass was broken only by low-growing bushes of alpenroses. The rays of the sun beat down unhindered and Joan felt inclined to be thankful for her shady hat.

She and Rosamund went along mainly in silence, since Joan's French was a completely minus quantity and Rosamund's not much better. Joan was beginning to wonder how on earth she was going to manage in lessons. For that matter, how did Rosamund manage? She decided to find out and poked her silent partner.

"How d'ye do in lessons?" she muttered.

Rosamund flushed, but shook her head. "Parlez en français," she muttered. "We must—I mean, il faut!"

Joan bestowed a curious look on her but said no more, and they finally reached the form room of IVa without her learning anything more.

The first lesson was arithmetic and Miss Wilmot, a

plump, pretty person, arrived to take a lesson in recurring decimals with them. She spoke French fluently, and like Biddy O'Ryan and several more of them, she was an Old Girl of the school. She revised the teaching of an earlier lesson, set the girls to working examples of the rule and then turned her attention to the newest new girl.

By this time Joan was becoming irritated, and she was worse because Rosamund so clearly strained every nerve to understand what was being said. Miss Wilmot sat down beside her and proceeded to try to find out how much she had grasped. She found it uphill work, for Joan was so blankly ignorant of French that almost every word had to be translated for her and her answers were given—very sulkily—in English which had to be turned into French and she requested to repeat them.

If this had happened at St. Matthew's, Joan would have "cheeked" her, but at first she didn't quite dare. For one thing, she missed the admiring looks and giggles which had frequently followed at her old school. Here, the girls simply went on with their work and took no notice. For another, there was something about Miss Wilmot, pleasant as she was, which kept the girl well in check at the beginning. The only one who appeared to mind was poor Rosamund whose cheeks burned as she bent over her work. As Joan sat next to her, she could not help hearing one or two of that young person's replies, and as they went on they grew nearer and nearer to sheer impudence.

Miss Wilmot took it very well. She never altered her quiet manner. But at last Joan, mistaking her manner for weakness, retorted to a question with a piece of impudence that made Rosamund cringe and those of the others who heard it yearn to get up and give the new girl a good shaking. She wasn't even funny. She was, as Len Maynard said later, merely downright rude.

Miss Wilmot had been showing Joan the working of the rule and ended with a friendly, "Now do you understand?"

"Not me!" Joan returned. "But don't disturb yourself. I couldn't care less!"

Nancy Wilmot was an easy-going creature, but this was

more than even she was prepared to stand. Still speaking in French, she said with great dignity, "I think you forget yourself and don't realise how rude you are. I see no reason to waste my time over anyone so rude and ungrateful. Take your books and go out of the room and wait in the corridor till I send for you." Joan hesitated and the mistress added in a voice which made the rest jump. "Be quick, please! You have wasted quite enough of our time this morning. Leave the room at once!'"

There was no mistaking either tone or gesture. Joan went even redder than Rosamund. To be sent out of the room like a naughty baby! And before all those other girls *and* Ros Lilley! For a moment longer Joan was tempted to defy the mistress and stay where she was, but she got such a look as took all the impudence out of her. She meekly picked up her books and left the room.

The form paid no apparent attention to her, but kept their eyes on their work. Miss Wilmot waited until she had gone and then began to correct what they had done. But there was that about her which warned them all to be careful. It was seldom that Miss Wilmot was anything but cheery, but now she was clearly furious. The way she slashed her pencil through mistakes. It was just as well that there were only ten minutes of the lesson left and more than one heaved a deep sigh of relief when the bell rang and, after setting an unmerciful amount of preparation, she gathered up her belongings and departed for a session with VIa during which she cooled down.

There was no chance for anyone to say anything about Joan, for Miss O'Ryan was waiting at the door when Miss Wilmot came out and she went in at once with a very subdued Joan trailing after her. Nor did that young woman give more trouble that morning. It is to be doubted if she learned much of the lessons themselves, but she did learn one or two phrases in French. Furthermore, she decided that perhaps she had better feel her feet a little before she behaved like that to any other mistress.

As for the girls themselves, they merely treated the affair as if it had never been. Joan was one of the people who can go to almost any length provided they have an admiring audience. She certainly did not have it in IVa and she behaved very well for her. Rosamund gradually recovered herself and, as she was anxious to do well and learn to speak both French and German as soon as possible, she gradually forgot the disturbance of the first lesson.

In the afternoon they had tennis together with Upper IVb. Tennis was something Joan had played occasionally on the public courts at Meadowfield and she had a rough and ready notion of the game, though her style was terrible. She foot-faulted, skied her balls, sent them out of court and into the net and held her racquet all wrong; but Miss Burnett, watching her, thought that with strenuous coaching she might make a player. She had plenty of strength, and once she had been got out of her faults ought to do well. Rosamund was still at the nursery stage. Carola Johnstone took her over, together with one or two other people who were little better and she and Joan saw nothing of each other for the whole afternoon.

Joan had no objection to learning the French for tennis terms. She liked the game and enjoyed herself thoroughly. By the time the hour had ended she was in high good humour and went off to join a little coaching class held by Mdlle for half-a-dozen girls who knew little or no French and really did her best. Rosamund was not in it as she was already being coached by Mdlle Berné from St. Mildred's, so went off to preparation with the rest.

Under vivacious little Mdlle de Lachennais, Joan found herself picking up a number of words though she inwardly mocked at the way Mdlle insisted on their pronouncing the said words. Still, she did learn and, when the lesson ended, she had decided that perhaps it would be as well to make every use of what she could pick up.

"Ros Lilley seems to be able to do it," she thought as she went upstairs to change out of tennis shorts and shirt into her cotton frock, "and if she can, I can! Shouldn't wonder if I managed better than her if it comes to that! I've a jolly good mind to do it! That 'ud show old Mother Gay who ought to have had her blinking scholarship!"

That scholarship still stuck in her throat. If she had been honest with herself, she would have owned that she was still wildly envious of Rosamund's winning it. She got round this by telling herself that it was all favouritism on Mrs. Gay's part and anyway, who wanted to be a "charity" schoolgirl? Her dad was *paying* for her and she was as good as anyone else. But she wasn't going to be beaten by anyone who was at the school through charity, so she had better make up her mind to work really hard. She had plenty of brains. Hadn't she led most of the other girls at St. Matthew's? If she applied that to lessons, she ought soon to be soaring far ahead of young Ros who had only been a hanger-on of her own.

What Joan forgot was that unless you have a solid foundation, you can't hope to build much of an edifice. Nor, if you have slacked all your school life, can you hope to turn to and work at fourteen and find it easy. At least it was better than applying her wits to rudeness to the staff. But she had a long way to go before she could become the sort of girl who was a leader in the Chalet School.

CHAPTER XI

MARY-LOU MAKES A DECISION

"PENNY for them, Mary-Lou!"

Mary-Lou looked up with a grin. "Not worth it! You can have 'em free gratis and for nothing if you want 'em."

Nina Rutherford came and sat down in the desk next to Mary-Lou's. "I don't want them if you'd rather keep them to yourself. Only it's not like you to sit staring at nothing for five minutes on end."

"Oh, I don't mind," Mary-Lou said largely. "I was just thinking about those two new Middles we've had wished on to us this term—Rosamund Lilley and Joan Baker. They're by way of being a problem, aren't they?"

"Joan Baker certainly is," Nina said with decision. "I rather like what I've seen of Rosamund Lilley."

"I agree with you. You know," Mary-Lou went on confidentially, "it's a mystery to me how two girls who have come from the same school can be so totally different. Rosamund *is* a decent kid when you can get through her shyness and reserve. But Joan Baker! I wouldn't have her as a gift with a pound of tea—not with a *ton* of tea. Remember that first night when she was landed on us? You could have cleaned her face with a knife and did you ever see anything more ghastly than that frock she wore?"

Nina unexpectedly chuckled. "You never saw the kit I wore to travel to England from Maggiore! Poor Cousin Guy! I don't wonder he looked horrified!"

"What was wrong with it?" Mary-Lou asked, shelving the question of the two new girls for the time being.

"It was black, to start off with—Continental mourning, you know, with rows of crape on the skirt and bodice. Signora Pecci had got it for me when—Oh, well, never mind that! She got it for me. I looked a complete freak. I didn't realise it at the time, but I must have been an awful shock all round." She laughed again and then asked, "Didn't Hilary or Vi tell you what I looked like?"

"Never said a word to me," Mary-Lou replied. "I don't suppose they thought much about it, anyhow. I'd had that accident at the end of the Christmas term and was *non est*, for weeks on end. They were too thankful to see me in one piece when we next met to bother about what anyone else looked like. I rather gathered they'd expected to find me bald, if not bandaged to the eyebrows, and hobbling about on crutches! Vi told me it was the relief of her life to find me more or less normal."

Nina joined in her laughter before she said, "Well, I looked an awful freak. I grant you it wasn't anything like Joan Baker's dress. Why did her people let her choose it? Her own mother might have worn it!"

"I've no idea. I should think, though, she was glad Matey put her foot down on it and made her get frocks like the rest of us. I can't," quoth Mary-Lou, "imagine anything more awful than being an outsider!"

"From what I've heard Joan was indignant about it," Nina said. "I overheard her holding forth to Betty Landon and one or two more and saying that it was too much to be expected to go back to baby frocks at *her* age!" She flipped open her manuscript book and made a face at the exercises in figured bass awaiting her there.

Mary-Lou craned over. "What a weird-looking mess!"

"And it's every bit as bad as it looks," Nina said ruefully. "Mr. Denny is a dear, but he thinks up the most awful figured basses. And it's so hard to remember not to use consecutive fifths in an exercise. I like them, myself."

"Oh, well, it's all Greek to me," returned Mary-Lou. "Better get down to it, my dear. *I've* got some very sticky German translation to do and as I can't find anything that looks like a predicate anywhere in the first sentence, I can't make much sense of it—so far. It'll take me all my time to produce something that'll pass muster with Sally-Go-Round-the-Moon. That's why I came in to prep early," she added as she picked up her pen with a resigned air.

It was Nina's turn to crane. She laughed when she saw what her friend had made of the first sentence. "No wonder!" she said. "You look that through again and for goodness' sake don't go calling predicates adjectives! It's there, all right, if you'll only use your wits!"

"Oh, is *that* what's wrong?" Mary-Lou surveyed her rough work thoughtfully. Then she picked up her Schiller and went through the German again while Nina began roughing in her exercise and they talked no more.

Ten minutes later the bell rang for preparation and the others came in, and by the time the silence bell had rung everyone was hard at work. Once the period ended, work was over for the day and you might do no more that night. The Chalet School authorities insisted on this rule being rigidly adhered to. Too many of the girls were in the Oberland because of medical trouble in their families and, while work was strenuous in work time, out of that, everyone was supposed to relax and rest.

Thanks to Nina's hint, the German went fairly well and Mary-Lou put it aside with a heartfelt sigh of relief and plunged at her algebra which she found easy enough. When this was done, she was left with a couple of chapters of *Dombey and Son* to read for questioning. She had read the book for amusement more than once, so she merely skimmed the pages. Then she shut it up, though she kept her rough book open before her in case anyone should come in with a right to ask what she was doing, and gave up her mind to the school's latest problem.

It was just a fortnight since Joan Baker had arrived at

the school, and in that time she had contrived to annoy every mistress and set the entire form by the ear, not to speak of making every last one of the prefects vow that she was worse than even Emerence Hope, the school's Bad Girl, had ever been. She was sticking to her resolve to learn as much French and German as she could while she was in the Oberland. She had settled on becoming a private secretary and she knew that if you could offer more than one language, you stood a much better chance of a good job. But she gave as little attention as she dared to lessons. She had quickly found that she had not the faintest idea of things that the other girls had absorbed earlier in their school life and she had no idea how to find them out. Neither had she the least idea of how to work. She hated the hour and a half of preparation they had every school day because she found it impossible to concentrate for longer than a few minutes. The result was that she fidgeted, looked round, scribbled all over her rough book and drove not only whoever was on duty to distraction, but her form mates as well.

Betsy Lucy had turned her out of the room the evening before, and when, after prep, she informed the new girl that she was to come back after Abendessen and make up the half-hour she had just lost, Joan had calmly defied her.

Betsy, like every other prefect, preferred to settle her difficulties for herself. On this occasion, however, she felt that it was beyond her and told Joan that she could either do as she was told or take a Head's Report.

Joan grinned impudently before she remarked, "So you know you can't make me? O.K. Go ahead and tell the Head tales if you feel that way—sneak!"

Betsy had been dumb with surprise for a moment. Then she recovered herself.

"Oh," she said crisply. "*I* shan't do the reporting. You'll do it yourself."

"Garn!" said Joan vulgarly. "Think I was born yesterday?"

"Yes," Betsy retorted. "So far as this school is concerned, I certainly do. You'll go to the study—*now*. You can say I've sent you to report yourself for impertinence and making a nuisance of yourself to everyone else in prep.

And if you don't go," she added, seeing the defiance in Joan's eye, "I shall certainly report you myself."

It had come to that, however. Joan had flatly refused to go to Miss Annersley and Betsy had, reluctantly, been obliged to go to report her as she had threatened. The Head asked one or two trenchant questions and then dismissed her with the remark that it was out of her hands now and she was to worry about it no more.

"I think Joan hardly realises what a serious thing it is to behave in this way to a prefect," she observed. "We must impress it on her that such things aren't done here with impunity. You were quite right to report her, Betsy, and would have failed in your duty if you had not."

Betsy departed, greatly relieved, and the Head went off to consult Miss Wilson, her partner. Between them, they planned out a course that might be hoped to put a stop to further ebullitions of this kind from Joan. As a result, when Abendessen was over and they were standing for Grace, Miss Annersley said quietly, "I wish to see Joan Baker in the study. Follow me, Joan, after Grace."

Even Joan could hardly defy the Head. She went along to the study feeling apprehensive. Arrived there, she had every reason to regret her behaviour before the Head had finished with her. Miss Annersley questioned her severely about the affair and though Joan might try to evade the questions, she found it impossible. In ten minutes' time the Head was in full possession of the facts.

"I see," she said. "Well, I don't suppose you need me to tell you that your conduct would be a disgrace to the most untrained urchin. You have disgraced not only yourself, but your parents and your former school. In future, please try to remember that we expect our girls to behave like gentlewomen. You will apologise to Betsy Lucy for your rudeness to her and, for the whole of next week you will forfeit your privileges."

"I don't know what you mean," Joan muttered, feeling impressed. Miss Annersley's voice had its most cutting tone and Joan was not too thick-skinned to feel that.

"I mean," the Head said, still icily, "that in your free time, you will not use the tennis courts nor be allowed to go rambles. Instead, you will take walks with one of the mistresses. You may not use the library—your present book must be handed in to the librarian who will retain it until the week is ended. You will be given a stamp for your home letter and collection money for church—by the mistress beside whom you will be sitting at the services. Apart from that you will have no pocket money this week. Finally, instead of enjoying the Saturday evening dancing and games, you will come to me after you have changed and I will give you something to do."

Joan was appalled by this. She had really had no idea what a Head's Report meant and such a comprehensive punishment nearly overwhelmed her. She wished she had tried to control herself and not answered the Head Girl so rudely. Miss Annersley waited to see if she had anything to say. Finding she had not, she touched the bell hanging over her desk. When one of the maids came to answer it, she was asked to find Miss Lucy and send her to the study. Margeli went off and the Head turned to her never-ending correspondence, leaving the culprit to wish she was anywhere else.

Betsy arrived and guessed what was to come. She flushed, but she held her head with dignity. In being so rude to her, Joan had challenged the entire prefect system at the Chalet School and an apology was justified.

"Joan has something to say to you, Betsy," Miss Annersley said gravely.

Betsy turned to Joan. She was a generous girl and, despite her ruffled feelings, she felt impelled to make things as easy for the new girl as she could.

Joan went scarlet. She didn't meet Betsy's eyes. Looking down, she mumbled, "I'm—sorry!"

"That's all right," Betsy said heartily. "It won't happen again, I'm sure." She turned an imploring look on the Head who nodded.

"That's all I want you for, dear. You may go."

"Thank you!" Betsy curtsied and fled and Joan was left with the Head.

"You will go to bed now," that lady said, determined to put a stop to this sort of thing once for all. "I will ring Matron Henschell so that she will know why you are coming so soon. Good-night, Joan. I hope you will not have to come to me again for this kind of behaviour."

"G-good-night! " Joan muttered. She managed to remember her curtsy as she reached the door. Then she fled. Since Matron was to be told she was coming, she had to go straight to St. Agnes; but she met Len Maynard on the way, and from the look Len gave her she guessed that the others knew something of what had happened and she hated it. She got to bed as fast as she could and cried herself to sleep. On the day on which Mary-Lou had been meditating over her attitude to the school at large and the prefects in particular, she had gone about like an outsize in thunderclouds. Hilary Bennet had demanded her library book after Frühstück, and when the rest went to tennis she was sent for a walk with Matron Gould to the Elisehütte where Nina's people were living at present to be with their own eldest girl.

Most of the Upper IVa left her alone. They had no real idea of what had happened between her and Betsy, for the latter had kept the affair to herself, but they knew well enough that Joan had been given a Head's Report and could guess that she must have been impudent to the Head Girl. They might and often were at loggerheads with that important body, the prefects, but they were not prepared to condone downright rudeness. Besides, thanks to Joan's antics the previous night, quite a number of them had been unable to work properly and what the staff had had to say had hardened their resolve to show Joan Baker that conduct of that kind just wouldn't do.

Rosamund, dimly feeling that she ought to help Joan, made a few remarks to her but was snapped at so perseveringly, that she gave it up and sheered off. She told herself that it was no good and she could only wonder that she had thought so much of Joan in the old days.

The climax had come at the end of the afternoon when Upper IVa had a period for essay-writing during which they were left to themselves and trusted to work steadily. Joan made herself most objectionable by scraping her chair backwards and forwards on the polished floor—shaking her pen until she contrived to bespatter the girl immediately in front of her, and yawning loudly and frequently. Yawning is infectious and before she was done she had half the form yawning with her. Very little essay was done by anyone and, at the end of the afternoon, Upper IVa told her what they thought of her and none of it was pleasant. Joan was furious and retorted with a will. So much noise was made that Mary-Lou, passing the door, went in under the impression that the form was conducting a free fight. Miss O'Ryan also passing went after her and they arrived in time to hear Joan swear vehemently at Alicia Leonard.

Miss O'Ryan ordered the rest of the girls off to change at once. Then she turned to Joan.

"You know," she said conversationally, "if you had been one of the Juniors, I should have marched you upstairs and washed your mouth out with soap and water. You are rather big for such treatment, however, but," her voice suddenly became severe, "for the rest of the day, you are in silence. Let us see if not speaking at all will help you to remember that there are certain words that schoolgirls may not use." She paused, but Joan had nothing to say. The history mistress wound up with, "if ever I hear of you using such language again, you will get a Head's Report. That will do now. You may go."

Joan went, but as she went, she made up her mind to guard her tongue for the future.

Mary-Lou had worried about the affair. It was bad enough talking like that in front of Upper IVa. They were mainly old enough to have some sense and she knew that they had all been horrified at Joan's language.

"But supposing she used expressions like that before the kids!" Mary-Lou thought. "Some of those foreign kids might use them and there'd be a nice how-d'ye-do!"

All this was passing through her mind as she sat with *Dombey and Son* before her, a pencil in one hand and the other running its fingers through her hair. She was so deep in thought that she never heard the bell ring for the end of prep and her own friends regarded her with amazement when they saw her still sitting there, her short curls all on end.

"What's biting you, Mary-Lou?" Hilary Bennet asked.

Mary-Lou looked at her vacantly. "What did you say?"

"I asked what was biting you. You're all right, aren't you?" Hilary regarded her with some alarm.

Mary-Lou came to herself with a run. "Of course I'm all right! There's nothing whatsoever the matter with me. I was only thinking."

"Well, don't overstrain yourself, whatever you do!" jeered Vi Lucy, relieved to see that Mary-Lou had recovered her usual manner. "Remember your brains had quite a nasty knock the term before last."

"Don't you worry!" her friend retorted. "I'm not you. *Your* brains might be affected, but mine can stand up to a thing like a knock." Then she changed her tone. "Seriously, I've got rather a problem to chew at."

Nina who had been scribbling madly at the last paragraph of her French essay, wrote the last word and then looked up. "Still worrying about that little idiot, Joan Baker? Don't you do it Mary-Lou! It's not your job."

"Oh, that's it, is it?" put in Lesley Malcolm. "Nina's right. It *isn't* your job—though I can't say that I think *that* fact will make you think better of it," she added. "If ever there was a champion butter-in in this school, it's you. At the moment. may I suggest that the bell has rung and we ought to be out of here?"

"Goodness! I never heard it!" Mary-Lou shuffled her books together, shot them into her desk and slammed the lid down. "Come on, Nina! Will you make a fourth with Hilary and Vi and me for tennis after Abendessen?"

"Doesn't Lesley want to play?" Nina asked.

Lesley shook her head. "Bill has invited a few of us to go mothing with her. Make up their set if you can, Nina. You haven't had much exercise today, have you?"

"Not with Plato demanding me this afternoon. He won't want me tomorrow, so I've the whole morning until my music lesson. Thanks, Mary-Lou. I'll love to play."

"Good! Vi's booked Number Four court. Katharine and Co. want it at twenty o'clock, so scram when Abendessen's over, will you? We shan't have too much time."

Nina nodded, laughed, and put her work away. Then they all trouped off to tidy themselves for Abendessen.

Mary-Lou played well for she hated to be second-rate in anything, but a good deal of the time her mind kept turning to the school's latest problem. When the set was over and the four of them were strolling back, Len Maynard came up to them. Rosamund was with her and Rosamund looked very pleased and excited.

"Oh, Mary-Lou," Len said, "Mamma's just been here and she says she's going to Montreux—to stay with your cousins, Nina—and taking the kids. She's going down early tomorrow morning and Papa's following after Mittagessen and they won't be back till Sunday evening. So no one will want the tennis courts and she said we three could ask anyone we liked to come and play in the afternoon as we haven't anything special on ourselves—and I wondered if you'd like to come and bring three other people? Con and I are having Rosamund and Prunella. Margot doesn't want anyone because their form are having a picnic, so she and Emmy won't be there. Anna will give us tea—real tea, I mean. Do come!"

"Thanks a lot," Mary-Lou said instantly. "Did you say Aunt Joey would be away for the week-end, Len?"

"Yes, but she'll be back on Sunday," Len replied. "You could get leave to go and see her then. Maria's going to Basle for the whole week-end to stay with Tant Frieda so Mamma will have to see to the babies herself."

Mary-Lou looked relieved. During the tennis practice she had made up her mind to apply to Joey Maynard for advice, and it had been a distinct blow to hear that she was going to be away. However, it would be much easier to have a long confidential chat on Sunday evening.

She bethought herself of one thing. "What does the Head say?" she asked.

"Oh, that's all right. Mamma said she'd told her and Auntie Hil—I mean the Head—said it would be all right if we had someone older with us. That," added Len frankly, "is one reason why I asked you. Oh, and I wondered if you'd look at Rosamund and tell us if she's going on all right. Prunella thinks she is, but we thought we'd like to have someone out of the Tennis Six to vet her."

Mary-Lou laughed and gave the crimson Rosamund an encouraging pat on the back. "With all the pleasure in life! Shall I go to the Head, Len?"

"Well, p'raps you'd better," Len agreed. "But I know it'll be O.K."

"Sure to be if Aunt Joey fixed it up with her more or less," Mary-Lou assented. "Still, it would be only decent. All right; I'll go. I suppose we hop over after rest tomorrow afternoon?"

"That's what Mamma said. Oh, goody, goody! We couldn't have gone, even with Prunella, if you hadn't agreed. But you're Va and you'll be VI next term and probably a prefect. The Head'll agree all right now!"

Mary-Lou chuckled as she turned to go and make herself fit to be seen before seeking out Miss Annersley to get official approval of the plan. She felt quite relieved. And she was sure that Aunt Joey would be able to advise her how to deal with Joan Baker and her vagaries, so *that* was all right, too.

CHAPTER XII

MARY-LOU SEEKS ADVICE

MARY-LOU asked for and obtained permission to go over to Freudesheim on the Sunday evening. She got it the more easily that there was to be no evening service at either the little chapel close by the gates of the big Sanatorium at the other end of the Görnetz Platz or in the tiny Catholic church, midway between the two main buildings on the shelf. The two Heads had decided that as it was a day of blazing heat, the girls might wander where they chose after Kaffee und Kuchen so long as they kept to the Platz, were in groups of not less than six girls, and remembered that it *was* Sunday. The Juniors were settled by Betsy Lucy and Co. inviting them to a picnic in the pine woods above the shelf and the rest were merely put on their honour to keep to bounds and good behaviour.

One girl was, of necessity, out of all this. Joan had forfeited all her privileges for the week and therefore might not leave the school grounds. Moreover, she had to be in charge of the duty mistress—Miss Derwent, in this instance. Miss Derwent was annoyed at having to have the responsibility and she gave Joan short shrift. She handed her a book, desired her to fetch her knitting or embroidery, and then marched her to the small plot sacred to the staff and ordered her to set up her deckchair there and stay there. The better to ensure that the girl did so, she settled herself and her own friends under the big walnut tree by the entrance. The garden was surrounded by a thick hedge, so Joan was unable to escape.

Mary-Lou enjoyed her afternoon, lounging under a group of larches at the far end of the garden, with the eleven or so other people who had formed what was called The Gang. They were not all quite so close as they had been, for Mary-Lou, Vi Lucy, Hilary Bennet and Lesley Malcolm were all in Va now; seven of the others were ornaments of Vb and the last, Jo Scott, was still a Middle and in Upper IVa. They all knew that the five in Va would be in one or other of the two Sixths next term and Mary-Lou and Lesley would certainly be sub-prefects if they were not full-blown prefects. But they still came together when they could.

The staff had also recognised that the little body of girls who had led the others during their Middles days must begin to branch away and had watched it happen with some trepidation. Sentimentality was frowned on in the school, and it would have been hard for anyone to try it on with Mary-Lou and one or two of the others; but there *were* girls who might have tried to cling to the old ways. But Mary-Lou still kept her hand on the reins and Mary-Lou had her head very well screwed on. It had come about without any fuss, whatever anyone might feel privately, and already those who had kept together during their earlier years, were parting just a little and spreading their own ideals and principles among the others.

However, on an off-day like this, The Gang came together and thoroughly enjoyed themselves. Kaffee und Kuchen was carried out and they had it in peace. Then came the orders for strolls, and Mary-Lou, refusing all invitations, went to the Fifth Form Splashery, saw that she was as spick and span as she could be, and slipped off through the gate in the hedge that divided the grounds of the Chalet School from the garden at Freudesheim.

It was early yet, but she knew that Joey kept her small fry to early bedtime so she went across the side lawn to the french windows of the Saal. All was quiet, though she could hear Anna singing in the back garden, and from the far side of the house, Rösli, known as the Coadjutor, was playing with Mrs. Maynard's St. Bernard, Bruno.

"They haven't got back yet," she thought, "or Bruno would be all over Aunt Joey. I can sit down and wait." And she dropped down on the step leading up to the open french window and leaned comfortably against the wall.

She became immersed in thought and paid no heed to the sound of a car stopping outside the Freudesheim gate. Neither did she see the tall fair man who came across the front lawn until she heard him whistling. She looked up. Then, with a cry of, "Uncle Jack!" she raced over the grass to fling her arms round his neck.

"Steady! Prepare to repel boarders!" he exclaimed. "What a weight you are when you do that, Mary-Lou! Well, what are you doing here, may I ask?"

"It's all right! The Head said I might. But—where's Aunt Joey and the kids?"

"Staying down at Montreux for the rest of the week."

"What? Oh, Uncle Jack! What a complete nuisance! Why on earth is she doing that?"

"Winnie Embury had to be rushed to hospital this morning with an acute appendix. Joey promised to stay and look after the kids until they can fix up with someone to come and take hold. You couldn't leave two demons like Paul and Robin to the care of maids and young Alan isn't much better. Poor old Winnie was in a regular stew when she could think for pain, so Joey offered to remain for the time being. It was a big relief to her. And she was bad enough without having to worry about those imps of hers."

"Yes, I see." But Mary-Lou's face remained clouded.

"What's eating you?" he demanded, eyeing her with curiosity. "Why do you want your Aunt Joey so urgently? Nothing wrong, is there?"

"Oh, no! At least—well, I want some advice."

"Oho! And what may you have been up to?"

"Oh, it isn't me," Mary-Lou told him, casting grammar to the winds.

"Can't you ask one of the mistresses—or the prefects?"

"No!" Mary-Lou was quite definite about this. "It concerns another girl, so I couldn't possibly go to either. As a matter of fact," she added calmly, "I'm butting in."

"I can't say that Joey's mantle has fallen on you for she still wears it—witness today's event! But you're following in her footsteps. She's a champion butter-in! Must you have advice now or can it wait a few days?"

"My own idea is the sooner the better. We don't want any really bad trouble in the school. I mean—well—we've never had any expulsions in my time——"

She got no further. At that moment Bruno, sensing somehow that Master, at least, had arrived, burst into the room, barking at the full pitch of powerful lungs and it was impossible to hear oneself speak. He hurled himself on Jack who reeled beneath the onslaught of several pounds of wildly-excited St. Bernard, and tried to wash his face.

Jack Maynard steadied himself with an effort and proceeded to calm down the almost hysterical creature.

"Down, Bruno! *Sit!* No; Missus isn't here. You'll have to do without her for the present. *Down!* Oh, Rösli," as the Coadjutor arrived, "bring us some lemonade and tell Anna that Madame will not be coming for a few days, but I'll be seeing her shortly. Shut *up*, Bruno! Quiet!"

At last Bruno decided to calm down. Rösli vanished to bring lemonade and Jack turned to his guest, saying, "You'd better let me hear more. Wait till the drinks come."

When the pair were settled with long frosty glasses of Anna's delicious home-made lemonade, and Bruno sitting heavily across Jack's feet, he turned to Mary-Lou.

"And now, Mary-Lou, what about it? Can I be any use, seeing Joey's not here?"

Mary-Lou sipped at her glass and then set it on the floor at the side of her chair where Bruno cocked a speculative eye at it, though he remained where he was for the moment. "You'll have to do, I suppose," she said.

"Get cracking, then, and tell me what all this is in aid of. You won't have too much time—in fact, I think you'd better stay to supper with me. I suppose Anna can provide. I'll go and give Miss Annersley a ring."

"I don't suppose for a minute she'll agree, but you can try if you like. No harm in trying. I hope she will, for I don't see how I can explain properly in just a few minutes and something will have to be done about it."

"Pessimist! I'll go and see what I can do."

He set his glass down on a table and went out to the hall where the telephone stood. There was an extension in Joey's study and another in her bedroom and a third in the room opposite which the doctor used. You could be private at any of these but, as Joey had once remarked, if you used the one in the hall, you might as well stand on the housetop and shriek your news to the Jungfrau for all the privacy you would get! He left the door wide open and Mary-Lou listened with all her ears to the scraps of talk she could hear.

"Yes; it's me and *only* me—Joey's staying down at Montreux until the end of the week. Winnie started an acute appendix at nine o'clock this morning. Oh, at once, of course. Revillier said when it was over that the thing burst in his hand. She's had a close shave—Yes; very bad, of course; they had to cut so deep."

At this point he paused, Miss Annersley having a good deal to say. Mary-Lou fidgeted. Then she heard him say, "Yes; she's here. I had to leave Jo down at Montreux. Martin thinks he can get hold of a cousin who'll come out and take hold in a few days' time. Meantime, as Joey was on the spot and is perfectly capable of dealing with even such rips as Paul and Robin, she's staying on for the present. Winnie's bonne can take charge of the babies."

There was another pause. Then he said, "Oh, I'm keeping her, if you don't mind. I'll hound her over in time for bed —What's that? Well, the fact is our Mary-Lou wanted advice from Joey and I've volunteered to take her place— Yes—Oh, rather!—Hilda, could you? I'll be just as glad to have Joey back again. Montreux's on the hot side at this time of year and I don't want either her or Cecil upset by excessive heat."

It was at this point that Mary-Lou's attention was distracted by a rough hairy body pressing against her legs and she turned round in time to see Bruno's nose in her glass while he lapped up the lemonade in short order.

"You awful dog!" she cried. "I'd only had about two laps at it! It serves you right if it makes you sick!"

Bruno looked up at her and wagged an ingratiating tail. "It's all very well," she scolded him, "but that was *my* nice cold drink. Oh, Uncle Jack!" as he returned to the Saal. "What's the effect of iced lemonade on a dog's tummy? Bruno's swiped most of mine."

"Serves you right for putting it where he could get at it," Jack said unsympathetically. "I don't suppose it'll do him any harm—cool him down nicely. You can go and get yourself another glass from the kitchen and don't start fussing. Bruno, my lad, you'd better go outside. If you want to be sick be sick on the lawn. Mary-Lou— you're spending the evening with me, so that's all right."

He turned Bruno out into the garden, very pleased with his nice cold drink, and Mary-Lou, to whom Freudesheim was a second home, departed for the kitchen and returned with a brimming glass which she carefully set down on the small table she pulled up beside her chair.

"And now," said Jack when she had settled herself again, "what is all this in aid of?"

Mary-Lou wriggled. "It's hard to begin," she said. We got a new kid after the beginning of term—Joan Baker."

"I thought she was called Rosamund Lilley?"

"Oh, we have her as well. This is another. They used to go to the same school in England, I gather. I suppose that's why Joan was landed on us."

"Ah! Well, what's wrong with her?"

"Now you're asking! She's *the* world's worst ass and if she goes on as she's been doing, she's going to be landed. That would be a—a *beastly* thing to happen! Rosamund's tried to help her. She's an awfully decent kid herself, but she's not very likely to have much influence over Joan. I should have said it might be the other way about," said Mary-Lou, who had a habit of startling her elders by her unexpected perspicacity.

Jack regarded her thoughtfully. "So you're going to take a hand yourself, are you? I seem to remember you plunged in on it with that kid—What's-her-name?—Jessica

113

Wayne, isn't it? After straightening out that young woman, why can't you handle Joan Baker?"

"That was quite different," Mary-Lou said slowly. "Jessica was off on the wrong foot and full of mad ideas, and she was eaten up with jealousy, too, poor kid. Once she got over that and began to see straight, I didn't have to bother about her—or not particularly. She straightened herself out. Joan—well, it's different. I don't see what or who she's got to be jealous about. It's—it's—oh, it's so *difficult*! " she broke off suddenly. "It sounds so *snobby*, and I'm *not* a snob and don't want to sound like one."

"O.K. You can cut that out. We'll take it as read. I'm not very likely to misjudge you, Mary-Lou. I've known you since you were a brat of nine or thereabouts! "

She gave him a fleeting grin. Then she sobered. "I'll do the best I can. The fact of the matter, Uncle Jack, is that Joan isn't—well—what Gran would have called 'a lady'. I don't mean she eats with her knife or anything like that, though her language could do with improvement. It's more in her mind. She has cheap ideas."

"In what way?"

"Well—she talks—about—*boys*! " Mary-Lou was very red as she got this out.

"Ye-es. Well, I suppose she's that age."

"Oh, I know. But we *don't*, you know. We do have boy-friends, but it's not the same thing as Joan means."

"How d'you know she does?" he asked, giving her a curious glance. He couldn't imagine anyone talking to Mary-Lou in that strain—or not for long.

"Hilary heard her talking a whole lot of rot to those young asses, Ursula Vidler and Sarah Hewitson. They're gigglers at the best of times and Hilary said she felt like shaking the lot of them, she was so mad! You know, Uncle Jack, we've never gone in for sentimental bosh."

"What did she do? She didn't proceed to extremes?"

"Well hardly! Oh, she said she asked Ursula and Sarah if they'd like other people to hear the mush they were talking? Later, she got them alone and told them exactly what she thought of that sort of thing and what anyone decent would think. I don't think," Mary-Lou went on sedately, "that they've tried to do it again. But when she'd sent off those two, Joan went for her and told her she was pi and goody-goody. Everyone was interested in boys and you had to know quite a bit about them. And she said of course old maids like the Heads and the Staff had to talk against things like that, but any natural girl *liked* to. She was worrying in case Joan had got hold of some of the kids. She simply told her that if she ever heard her talking such unpleasant mush again she'd report her. Joan said she was a sneak and a Quisling and Hilary walked away and left her. But she told our lot and we've been keeping our ears open and I don't think it's happened again."

"I see. Hilary was quite right, of course. We all want you girls to have boy-chums as well as girls. You'll grow up lop-sided if you don't. Besides, a boy's outlook can be very good for a girl, just as a girl's outlook can be very good for a boy. But the sort of thing you whisper and giggle about is nasty, Mary-Lou. You're right there."

"Well, besides that, she acts as if prees and staff were your natural enemies. She had a turn-up with Betsy Lucy and cheeked her all ends up. And before that, so Jo Scott told me, she'd cheeked Miss Wilmot until she got herself sent out of the room. The rest of IVa seem to have ticked her off about it—after all, we all *like* Miss Wilmot; she's great fun out of school and quite decent in—and Joan swore at them. I heard her myself. It was really bad language, Uncle Jack. Miss O'Ryan heard her and put her into silence for it and also, I think, told her off."

"I can imagine it," he said drily. "Well? Go on!"

"Oh, it's all that sort of thing! And you know, Uncle Jack, if she goes on, there's going to be a most terrific bust up about it. No Head would stand for that sort of thing. The thing is, what can we do about it? I don't think that it's much use trying to talk to Joan."

"No; I shouldn't think so," he agreed. He looked at her thoughtfully. Mary-Lou might be only fifteen, but she was very grown-up in many ways—though not in Joan Baker's sense. He decided he would talk straight to her.

"You've got to remember one thing, my child, and that is that I rather think Joan belongs to people who finish school at fifteen. That means that they *are* much more grown-up about that sort of thing than most of you girls

115

who expect to stay at school for at least another two years with two or three years of training to follow. In consequence, you give your minds to games, lessons and things of that kind. You are much younger there, than girls like Joan. Make allowances for that fact."

Mary-Lou nodded, watching him with wide blue eyes.

"So far as cheeking people is concerned," he went on, "I don't think you need worry. By the time term ends she'll have found that no one at the Chalet School admires that sort of thing. She'll probably have the sense to see it won't do and stop it of her own accord."

"I'm sure I hope she does," Mary-Lou returned. "Young Emerence, did, of course."

"Now for helping her. The best advice I can give you is to try to let her know that you have a friendly feeling for her. It's no use preaching what is or isn't done in the school. You'll only put her back up. But try to make her feel that you can be a friend in need and you may get some sort of hold on her. Is there anything particular she's interested in that you could join in with her?"

"She's quite keen on tennis," Mary-Lou began. Then she gave a wail. "Oh, Uncle Jack! *Must* I start taking her on for that? I'm in the Six myself and need all my spare time for practice, not to mention the General Schools at the end of the term! It's going to take me all my time to keep going with that lot and what's left I wanted for just enjoying myself. If I've *got* to coach anyone I'd so much rather it was someone I really *liked*!"

"You don't have to do anything about it," he replied. "No one asked you to butt in. But if you do, then you'll find that you've got to make sacrifices somewhere. You asked for advice and I'm giving it. You needn't take it."

"That's where you're wrong. I can see for myself that if I take an interest in Joan's tennis it's just possible it may make all the difference to her. How can I stand out when anyhow I've decided to butt in?"

"You can't—not if I know you," he said. "You think it over. Only, if you're going to put the school first and Mary-Lou Trelawney's wishes last, it may mean the saving of Joan. From what you say, I should imagine that if, for any reason, the school decided they couldn't keep her, she might go from bad to worse."

"But that makes me responsible!" Mary-Lou exclaimed.

"I don't say it *will* happen. But it *might*. Mary-Lou we can't live for ourselves alone. We're bound to have some effect on everyone we contact, either good or bad."

"Oh, Uncle Jack! I never thought it went so far."

"You can take my word for it. It does! However, I'm giving you no orders."

"No; but you've left it to my conscience and that's just the same."

"Is it? I'm glad to hear it. My good kid, be thankful that you've had the sort of up-bringing that's given you a lively conscience. Come on to supper and then—well then, I'm afraid you'll have to go. Think it over, that's all."

He stood up, pulled her out of her chair and marched her off to the Speisesaal where Anna had left a delicious cold meal of chicken salad, stewed cherries floating round a mound of ice-cream and sponge-cake for them and saw to it that she made a good meal. When it was over, he left the local gossip with which they had amused themselves and reverted to the reason for her visit.

"I've just one thing more to say. Don't decide anything in a hurry. Once you begin, you must keep on."

"Oh, I quite see I'll have to do or have no peace! One thing, I can't do anything about it till the end of this week."

"How's that?"

"Joan's on Head's Report. She can't use the tennis courts out of actual games' time until that ends. I must just go ahead and make the most of it, for I can see I shall have to take the job on. You *say* you aren't ordering me to do anything, but you haven't really left me any choice."

"No; being you, I suppose I haven't. I'm sorry, Mary-Lou, but there it is. And now, glad as I am to have had your company, I'm going to push you out. You'll be late for Prayers if you don't go at once. Good-bye, my child! Best wishes for your crusade!" He bent to kiss her.

"You're rather a duck, Uncle Jack," she said. "Thanks for helping me—even if I don't like the way you've helped." She glanced at her watch. "Heavens! I doubt if

I can make it unless Prayers are late! My love to Aunt
Joey!"

The next moment she was flying over the lawn, her long
legs clearing the ground at a tremendous pace. He watched
her out of sight and then went to ring up his wife and tell
her the latest happenings at the Chalet School.

CHAPTER XIII

THE PREFECTS WAKE UP

"BETSY, what is at the bottom of Mary-Lou's latest?"

Betsy Lucy looked up from the anatomy notes she was
revising. "What's that? I wasn't paying attention."

"I asked you what you thought was at the bottom of
Mary-Lou's latest," repeated Katharine Gordon sitting
down on the arm of the big armchair in which Betsy was
sprawling, since it was Saturday afternoon and a fine
drizzle was falling which had put a stop to either games or
excursions. "My good girl, why are you swotting on a
Saturday afternoon? What price rules? You're breaking
them right and left, let me remind you! And you the
Head Girl! Really, Betsy! I'm ashamed of you!"

Betsy laughed. "How sad—how truly sad! I feel overwhelmed! Consider me to be casting dust and ashes on
my head if that'll make you feel any better!"

Katharine joined in her laughter. "What an ass you are!
No, but seriously; what *is* Mary-Lou up to?"

"In what way?"

"Well, she seems to be taking up that awful new kid,
Joan Baker. You know the Head sent her—I mean Mary-
Lou—to the Elisehütte with a message for the Ruther-
fords this morning? Well, I was there and Mary-Lou
asked if she might take Joan with her! And she speaks to
her whenever she meets her—I've seen her!"

"Why did the Head send Mary-Lou? What was wrong
with Nina going? After all, she's their cousin."

"Oh, wake up, do! As if you didn't know that Herr
von Eberhardt comes on Saturday mornings to give Nina
her piano lesson! You don't suppose the Abbess would

interrupt a special lesson just to send a note to someone? There were at least a dozen other people available, including Mary-Lou. *She* was sent—and she asked if she might take Joan. I want to know why."

"I wasn't thinking," Betsy confessed. "I've been swotting those wretched notes up till my brain feels all mushy, only it did seem a good chance to do a spot of revision. The nearer that awful exam comes, the less I feel I know."

"Well, you won't help matters by swotting yourself into brain fever," Katharine said unsympathetically. "You give it up and attend to me instead."

"But I can't help you. I haven't the foggiest idea what Mary-Lou is up to. How should I? She always had got away with things most of us wouldn't dream of. As for Joan Baker, she's welcome to her for all of me! It isn't often I take a deep dislike to anyone, but I don't mind telling you that if I heard Mary-Lou had gone to see her off to her own home for keeps it wouldn't break my heart!"

"I don't suppose it would," Katharine said drily. "Apart from her tennis which looks like being good after proper coaching, I can't say it would break mine. But what I'm getting at is what Mary-Lou is playing at. I should have said that if there *was* a girl she would avoid, it would be Joan. They're the absolute antithesis of each other——"

"The *what*?"

"Antithesis. And if you don't know what it means you ought to be ashamed of yourself! Go and find a dicker!"

Betsy laughed whole-heartedly. "Swallowed it, hook, line and sinker!" She sobered suddenly. "Oh, I know what you mean. Yes; that's rather an odd combination, isn't it? If it had been that other new kid, Rosamund Lilley, I could have understood it. She's quite a nice kid, if she doesn't seem to be outstanding in any one thing. But Joan Baker! No, Katt. That really is too much."

Sybil Russell, the only other girl in the room, had been sitting quietly, working at some elaborate embroidery. She looked up now to say, "It isn't, you know."

The other two turned and Katharine nearly fell off her perch. Betsy caught and steadied her, as she exclaimed, "Not? What do you mean, Sybs?"

119

Katharine removed herself to a chair and demanded, "What? I should say it was the last thing to be expected."

Sybil took a stitch or two before she replied. Then she laid her work in her lap for a moment to say, "Mummy says that Mary-Lou often reminds her of Auntie Jo when *she* was a kid. Oh, not in looks!" as the other two exclaimed. "In character! Auntie Joey's always been the butter-in of the family. Mummy says when she was at school if she saw a thing needed doing, she just waded in and did it regardless. Mary-Lou's a cat of the same colour."

Betsy and Katharine looked at each other. Katharine spoke first. "I wonder?" she said. "There's a lot in that."

Betsy crossed her knees and clasped her hands round them. "Joan Baker seems to me to be a thoroughly nasty piece of work. She's a giggler and worse. I can't see Mary-Lou, of all people, making a pal of her!"

"I never said that." Sybil took up her work again. "Well, what *do* you mean then?" Betsy demanded.

Katharine was quicker. "Are you trying to say that our one and only Mary-Lou has seen it and decided to take her in hand and—and bring her up the way she should go? You *do*! Well, even for Mary-Lou, that strikes me as being somewhat of a chore!"

"But," said Sybil, stitching away steadily, "isn't that just the sort of thing she *would* do?"

"Who would do what?" asked Carola Johnstone as she and two or three of the others came in. "What are you all talking about?" she added as she perched on the windowsill beside Sybil. "Sybs! Give us the benefit of your wisdom! We may as well get some good out of something."

"We were talking about Mary-Lou just then," Sybil said.

"What about her?" asked Amy Dunne, a plump, rosy-faced young person.

"I'll explain." And Katharine gave a brief résumé.

"Ye-es," Hilary Wilson said thoughtfully when she had finished. "We're all ready enough to help when it's pointed out to us; but Mary-Lou sees for herself and goes ahead. It's odd, because she's quite a bit younger than we are— not sixteen till July, is she? Sybs, you ought to know."

"Her birthday's in July," Sybil agreed. "I don't think it's odd, Hilary. Until she was ten she lived entirely with

Auntie Doris and her Gran. The only other girl she ever knew before she came to school was Clem Barrass and Clem is a good two years older than she is. I know both Mummy and Auntie Jo think it all helped to make her very grown-up in some ways. Perhaps that's one of them."

"It might be," Hilary said doubtfully. "All the same, you know, I feel rather a worm. *We* ought to be seeing what we can do about helping Joan to become a nicer girl, but we haven't even seen that we might do anything about it. It's taken Mary-Lou to do that."

"We're all awfully busy, especially this term with Higher in the offing," Carola pointed out.

But Hilary could think to some purpose herself, once she started. "But if you come to that, all that crowd has the General. They're just as busy as we are."

Sybil took it up again in her placid way.

"Isn't it just the sort of thing she *would* do? Think back to last Christmas term. What about Jessica Wayne? Who took her firmly in hand? And, you know Jessica is turning into a very decent girl. I've often thought that it was thanks to Mary-Lou and no one else."

"Oh, come, Sybil!" exclaimed Blossom Willoughby. "It's not *all* Mary-Lou! Give the school at large a little credit for it! I grant you Mary-Lou barged in first, but the influence of the school itself helped a lot."

"I'm not belittling that," Sybil replied as she rethreaded her needle with a fresh strand of silk. "Only it didn't have a chance until Mary-Lou pitched in and broke up the ice round Jessica. After that, of *course*, the school got going."

"And," put in Betsy, "what price young Verity? No one can say that Mary-Lou hasn't been the only thing more than once that has saved her from trouble. She's risked fusses on her own part, but she's stood firmly by Verity. And if she hadn't Verity would have been for it over and over again."

"Six and two threes," Hilary said. "Mary-Lou's kept Verity awake and Verity has kept Mary-Lou's feet on solid earth. It's true enough that she sees where help is needed and gets down to it. That's why I do feel a worm. Here's nearly half the term gone and we've just let Joan

Baker stew in her own juice and not done a thing about it."

"Well, what do you propose we should do?" Betsy demanded. "It's all very well to sit there tearing your hair and calling yourself a worm. What are you going to *do*?"

"There, as the charlady said when asked for a character, you *'ave* me!" Hilary confessed. "I haven't the foggiest!"

"I suppose," Katharine interjected, "that we ought to take an interest in the girl. Apart from her tennis which might be quite good if she was worked up, there's nothing I like about her. It'll take some doing on my part."

"But look here!" Blossom cried. "We're prefects! We can't go round making a fuss of one Middle. The rest *would* have something to natter about in that case!"

"I don't mean we should go out of our way to do it," Katharine replied. "But we might be as friendly as we are with a dozen or more of that lot. But I certainly think that, as prefects, we ought to be doing something about it ourselves and not leave it all to a brat like Mary-Lou."

"Do you think she'd pay any attention to us?" Betsy asked, looking troubled. "She seems to look on us as—as the troops of Midian where she's concerned."

"Isn't that to be expected from a Middle?" asked Amy.

"From kids of twelve and thirteen—yes. But Joan is nearly fifteen, I believe. I'm afraid I'm out of it where showing her my friendliness is concerned. She loathes me with a deadly hatred because I gave her that Head's Report. And yet I don't see what else I could have done."

"Oh, you were quite right," Katharine said quickly. "No girl could be allowed to get away with cheek of that kind. Don't you agree with me, folks?"

"Every time!" Blossom said. "Don't you worry. If you'd let her go then, she'd have tried it on, probably with something more outrageous next time. And then she'd have gone on to the staff and *then* she'd have been for it all right! Let's hope this week has taught her a lesson. I do agree we ought to keep our eyes open and see what she's about. She's not likely to do much harm with the crowd she's with now. But it mightn't be the same if she got hold of some of the kids."

"We certainly mustn't allow that," Betsy said sharply. "All right, Katt. You and Blossom between you can concentrate on her tennis and the rest of us must just look out for chances to show her that we *aren't* her natural enemies."

However, something was about to happen that put the whole thing out of their heads. It was heralded by a tap on the door and the entry of Margot Maynard.

"Please," she said, "the Head wants to see us all in Hall in ten minutes' time. I was to ask you to see that everyone is there and in her place."

"Oh? Very well, Margot. Thanks," Betsy replied.

Margot grinned and disappeared again, leaving the prefects to wonder aloud why the Head should want them in the middle of Saturday afternoon. Sybil folded up her work and put it away and Betsy tossed her anatomy notes into the cupboard. Then they went downstairs to Hall, where quite half the school was already assembled. A buzz of chatter greeted them, for everyone was curious as to why the Head wanted to see them at such a time. Why not leave it till Prayers that evening?

"I don't know any more than you," Betsy protested to Jean Ackroyd, the Second prefect, when that young woman accosted her. "We'll just have to wait till the Head arrives. And by that same token, we ought to be shushing those kids. They'll raise the roof if they go on like this. Shove that bunch from Lower IVb into their places and I'll get up on the platform and see what I can do about it."

Jean went to order the huddle of excited Junior Middles to their seats and Betsy, quickly threading her way between forms and clusters of chattering girls, mounted the platform and rang the bell on the reading-desk sharply. Silence fell almost at once and everyone turned to look.

"Yes!" she said. "I think you *had* better be a little quieter! Come in, you folk!" to a small group of girls from Vb who appeared in the doorway at the far end of the great room. "Get to your places and be quick about it! Emerence, go and sit down! You Juniors, settle yourselves. Do you all want the Head to come and find riot let loose? She'll have something to say in that event."

Recalled to their senses, the girls hurriedly took their

proper places and once she was sure that her words had worked properly, Betsy descended and went to her own place after telling them they might talk if they did it quietly.

"If you don't," she finished, "I hope you're all prepared to write out that speech of King Lear's about Cordelia's voice a dozen times. I could find better ways of spending Saturday afternoon myself!"

It was quite enough. The girls talked quietly among themselves, but always with one eye on the door, and when light footsteps warned them that the Head was coming, it was a very prim and proper gathering that heaved itself to its collective feet as she entered.

"Sit down, girls," she said when she was leaning on the reading desk. "I'm sorry to break into your Saturday afternoon, but I want to know how many of you expect to be visiting either relatives or friends at half-term."

About a score of people raised their hands. Half-term, so far as they knew, was not due for a fortnight yet. She counted them rapidly as did Miss Dene who had come with her. Then she nodded to them to sit back again.

"And now," she said, her beautiful voice ringing to the farthest benches, "I want to know how many people are expecting or wishing to take friends with them."

At least forty odd hands were raised. Jo Scott stood up, very pink in the face, and announced, "Please, Miss Annersley, I had a letter from Mummy this morning and she told me to ask if Prunella Davidson and Ruth Barnes and Maeve Bettany might come home with me?"

"By all means," Miss Annersley said. "Anyone else want more than one?"

Quite a dozen people did. A number of the girls had their homes in Switzerland and there were half-a-dozen Swiss girls in the school. Miss Dene quickly got details and then she and the Head conferred together for a minute or two while the school watched them, inwardly seething with curiosity. What *did* all this mean?

They heard in a minute or two. Miss Annersley laid her finger on the list her secretary had made, said something, and then Miss Dene left Hall and they heard her hurrying away across the entrance hall while the Head turned to her charges with a brilliant smile.

"Now, girls, we are obliged to move half-term to next week-end instead of the one after. This may make a difference to your plans, and we can't make ours until we know that all those who are expecting to be away really will be. You are to go to your form rooms where the prefects will bring you postcards to write this news to your people. Miss Dene is going down to Interlaken on the sixteen o'clock train and will post them there so that they reach your homes by Monday if possible. Betsy Lucy!"

Betsy stood up at once. "Yes, Miss Annersley?"

"I want you prefects to distribute the cards to the various forms, wait until they have finished writing and collect them again and take them to Miss Dene in the office. That is all. School—stand! Turn! Forward—march!"

They marched out smartly and went to their form rooms.

"What have we to explain to our people," Rosamund wanted to know. "I'm not going home or staying with anyone. Won't we just be at school?"

An immediate chorus answered her, but before she had managed to grasp what any of them were trying to tell her, Katharine arrived with their postcards. She gave them five minutes to write what they had to say, then sat down at the mistress's table to do her own.

"What are we to tell our folks?" Francie Wilford asked.

"Just that half-term will be next week instead of the week after and the school will be closed from Friday to Tuesday," Katharine replied.

"Where are we going?" came from all corners of the room at this.

"Some of you are going to friends or relatives, of course. The rest are off with the staff, but I can't say where, for I really don't know," Katharine replied with a glance at the card she was scribbling to an artist aunt who was at the Tiern See in Tirol, and to whom she was going with any luck. Katharine's Aunt Luce was a woolly-minded creature and there was no relying on her movements. "I expect the Head is waiting for the answers to these cards before she finally decides."

125

"Do you mean," Rosamund asked shyly, "that we may be going to see some of the lakes or the big cities?"

Katharine smiled at her. She was a tall girl with a dignified manner, by no means pretty, but with a distinction of bearing that impressed her juniors on most occasions. Besides, as they all knew, everyone expected that later on, she might be called on to represent her country at tennis. She was by far the finest player the school had ever had and unusually good for any schoolgirl. Rosamund had lately taken to regarding her with awe and admiration—from afar off. Sentimental grande passions were severely sat on at the Chalet School.

"Yes," she said. "It's bound to be something of that kind. But, as I said, we'll have to wait to know where. Now get on with your cards, please. If we make Miss Dene miss her train she'll have something to say!"

That was quite enough. Everyone set to work and the amount some of them contrived to squeeze into the limited space was amazing. As they finished they brought up their cards to the table and handed them to the prefect, who then dismissed them to their lawful occasions. Joan came one of the last. She laid down her card, but instead of going, she stood there, twisting her fingers. The prefect looked up, startled.

"Anything wrong?" she asked kindly.

"Will I—be let—go?" Joan asked gruffly with a very red face.

"Of course you will," Katharine replied. "You ought to enjoy it, Joan. This is your first visit abroad, isn't it?"

Joan nodded, turned away and left the room as Rosamund came up with hers. Katharine smiled at her.

"You ought to have a good time too," Katharine remarked. "We always do on these occasions. Off you go now! It isn't much longer till Kaffee und Kuchen."

Rosamund gave her an adoring look and went. Katharine never noticed it, for Maeve had arrived with her postcard and a string were following her.

The Maynards were not going home, of course, since their mother was away and no one seemed to know when she would return. Mr. Embury's cousin was already helping with a friend's family and would not be free for another fortnight. Joey, therefore, had insisted that she must stay. Winifred Embury had been very ill for though the operation had been a complete success, she had suffered badly from shock and it would be some time before she would be fit enough to take the reins again herself. The Embury home was outside Montreux, a little way up the mountain slope, and so much cooler than the lakeside. Joey and Baby Cecil were both thriving there and Mike, who had been lonely in the home nursery with only three babies, was enjoying life with Paul and Robin. Maria Marani had gone there, too. She was quite capable of dealing with even such imps as the Embury pair. As for the twins, they were happy with small Alan Embury and, as Joey had remarked during a telephone conversation with the Head, it all fitted in very nicely. But it did mean that the triplets might not go home. Their father was very busy at the big Sanatorium and Anna was taking advantage of her mistress's absence to have a good cleaning at Freudesheim. No one wanted three imps of nearly thirteen there!

"It's rotten luck," Len said to Rosamund. "Mamma said we could ask you and Emmy for half-term and now it's off. You'll just have to come next term instead."

"And I meant to write another story," Con put in mournfully. "I've got a gorgeous idea boiling up inside me!"

"Oh, well, it may give you an idea for something else," Len said soothingly. "Anyhow, you'll have to keep off it for this term, Con. You know we both want our remove." She giggled. "We ought to be Vb next term! It'll be a yell, won't it? We'll be Seniors in school. D'you think Matey will let us be Seniors out?"

"Sure she won't!" Con was positive on this point. "We aren't thirteen till November. Who ever heard of a Senior of twelve?"

Joan, who was lounging past, stopped. "Where are we likely to go?" she asked bluntly.

But that was something no one could tell her though they had a good deal of fun over making guesses. Someone else wondered if they would visit Basle which they had never seen properly as yet. Someone else was all for Neuchâtel. However, it was only guessing and they had to hold their horses until the Wednesday when, Prayers being over and the Catholics having joined the Protestants in Hall, Miss Annersley looked smilingly at the eager faces in the body of Hall and made an announcement that set them all agog once more.

"We have had replies to all your cards so now things can begin to move. Quite half you girls are going to friends or relatives. That leaves sixty-one of you to the school. You will be divided up into groups of ten each and one of eleven with one mistress and a prefect or two in charge and you will all go to different places. Miss Dene is busy typing out the lists now and she will put them up during the morning. Then you will see to which group you belong and where you are going. That is all I am going to tell you. I have only this to add. Our usual rule obtains, and any girl who neglects her work or behaves badly will be left behind at school. That is all."

She gave the signal to Miss Lawrence sitting at the piano, and the school marched out to the morning's work, all determined to do their best to avoid the awful penalty for bad work or behaviour which she had just pronounced and all in a pleasing state of anticipation.

CHAPTER XIV

TOOTHACHE—AND A GREAT SURPRISE

BEFORE half-term arrived Miss Annersley told the School that Mme de Bersac had had a second son. Some of the Sixth remembered her from their kindergarten days and most of them knew that Simone de Bersac was Joey Maynard's friend. They cheered when they heard the news and Betsy, speaking for them all, asked if a message of congratulation might be sent.

The result was that Simone telephoned and asked that the School might be given an extra day at half-term in honour of her little Jean. Naturally, the girls were thrilled and a special vote of thanks was passed to Simone and her son. Luckily the tourist season had hardly begun, so there was no difficulty in arranging with the various pensions and hotels where the girls who were not going to parents or friends would be staying.

The Maynard triplets were going to Basle, together with Rosamund, Emerence, Vi Lucy, Barbara Chester and Josette. With them were two prefects, Hilary Wilson and Sybil Russell, and the mistress in charge was Miss Wilmot. All of them rejoiced when Len read out the names to them.

Joan Baker was not included. She had been invited by Mary-Lou to go home with her, the reason given being to practise her tennis. Joan knew that the invitation was a great honour, but she was rather awed by it. She didn't guess that Mary-Lou's real reason was to continue with the resolve she had made after her conversation with Dr. Maynard, to do all she could to help Joan to become the kind of girl who would fit in with the rest of the school.

Basle is a very interesting city. The girls, as they explored it, learned a good deal of its history. On Friday afternoon they went to the open air baths which had been made in the Rhine and were amazed at the force of the current in the river.

They were staying in one of the suburbs at a pension kept by Frau Piguet, who had made them very welcome and given them a wonderful meal. But that night something happened which threatened to upset their plans.

Rosamund had spent part of Friday night awake with violent toothache. It had wakened her about eleven o'clock and for a good hour she had lain still, enduring as best she could. Then a sudden vicious dart of pain had ended that. She cried out, rousing Hilary Wilson in the bed next to hers.

Hilary had groped her way to the next bed where Rosamund was lying sobbing into her pillow, and demanded an explanation. When she got it, she had slipped on dressing-gown and bedroom slippers and gone to rout out Miss Wilmot.

Nancy Wilmot had fished her First Aid box out and padded along to the dormitory where she had ministered to a bad double tooth with cotton wool and oil of cloves. She had then dosed Rosamund with disprin and by two o'clock the pain, vanquished by this treatment, had let her drift off into an uneasy sleep.

In the morning Miss Wilmot demanded the name of

129

Frau Piguet's dentist and got an appointment for nine o'clock. He found Rosamund's tooth so badly gone that the only thing to do was to extract it. He was a skilful operator, but Rosamund was a highly strung girl, and by the time it was all over and she was back at Frau Piguet's, it was plain to everyone that she was certainly not fit for a day's sightseeing.

Miss Wilmot was in a quandary. She felt that she could hardly leave the girl alone for a whole day and yet it was hard on the others to penalise them for one. Finally Hilary made a suggestion. She would stay with Rosamund and Miss Wilmot could take the others as arranged.

Hilary was seventeen-and-a-half and a steady girl, with her head well screwed on. Rosamund had so far proved a law-abiding young thing and, in any case, was in no state to indulge in wild pranks at present.

"Have a quiet day, Hilary," the mistress said when they were outside the dormitory. "I'll give you some money and you can take Rosamund to the Rheinweg to that café if she feels well enough after a nap. If she seems all right I'd keep her out all the afternoon. The fresh air will be good for her. Have you any books with you? You might take them and sit in one of the parks or go up to Pfalz and sit there. Don't speak to any strangers and keep to the main streets. We'll be back around six o'clock. Your German is quite fluent—and you can always find someone who has a modicum of English." She paused; then she added, "You're *sure* you don't mind staying?"

"Not in the least," Hilary said cheerfully. "I'll remember, Miss Wilmot. I didn't bring any books and I don't suppose Rosamund did, either, but there are plenty of bookshops about and we can easily buy something."

"I'll make you a present of the books. And Hilary, on Monday we'll visit Augst and see those Roman remains of yours. Tomorrow will be a quiet day, of course, and it's nervous reaction that's wrong with Rosamund now. I've given her a disprin and she ought to get a good nap. Come to my room and I'll give you the money."

She counted out an ample supply and handed it over and then she had to hasten off to take the others to visit the Münster. They were late in starting and she had had to
130

ring up Biddy O'Ryan and explain that they would be an hour later than they had expected. Hoping that everything would be all right, she hurried her flock off and Hilary was left alone with the patient.

Rosamund slept until noon. When she woke up she was almost herself, though she owned to Hilary that she didn't feel up to any sightseeing. She was very upset because the prefect had lost it on her account, but Hilary only laughed and told her to get up and dress and they would be off to the Rheinweg to seek a meal.

"Then Willy's given me some money and we're to buy ourselves a book each. We'll hunt up some park or other and have a jolly afternoon reading," she said cheerily. As we have an extra day, anyhow, I'm not really missing anything. I'll give you ten minutes," she added as she went to the door, "and if you're not down by that time I'll come up after you. Heaven help you if I have to do that!" She ended with a gay laugh.

Rosamund laughed too, and rolled off the bed. She felt really much better. She spent two minutes in tidying the bed and took the rest to make herself trim.

"Hilary's a *dear*!" she thought to herself as she brushed out her long dark mane before the mirror and plaited it into a thick tail with deft fingers. "There!" She tossed it back over her shoulder, brought her hat and settled it neatly. "I'll do, I think. Where's my bag? Good! Now I'm ready! Have I clean hanky?" She had. "All O.K."

They caught their tram and reached the Hoheweg without trouble. Hilary chatted amiably, mostly about school affairs, and Rosamund found the last remnants of her shyness and fears slipping away never to return. They reached the café where they had been the day before and Hilary's German was quite equal to ordering the sort of meal that someone with a sore mouth could eat comfortably. Rosamund enjoyed the meal and Hilary found herself liking "this new kid" more and more.

"Well," Hilary said at last, "we'd better go and see about those books."

"What am I to do about choosing a book? I don't know enough German to read one."

"Oh, I expect we'll find English story books all right,"

131

Hilary replied readily. "And there's always the Tauchnitz editions if the worst comes to the worst. They're English books published by the Tauchnitz firm in paper covers for the use of tourists. I know we have a lot at home from the times when Dad's firm used to send him abroad. They do a lot of continental business. Come on and let's see what we can find."

In the big shop, they finally found an English section and Rosamund pounced triumphantly on a Josephine Bettany she had never read.

"Could I have this?" she implored. "I have some cash of my own if it's too dear."

Hilary laughed. "It's quite all right and it's a wizard yarn. I *know*! I have all Joey's books at home. Yes; take it. And I'll have this Angela Thirkell which certainly *is* beyond what Miss Wilmot gave us, but I can add the rest myself. Come on and pay for them and then we'll go up to the Pfalz. It'll be coolish so high up."

Rosamund was quite agreeable, so they paid their shot, left the shop and presently were climbing up the steep road to the Pfalz, a terrace behind the Münster, with chestnut trees making it shady and a glorious view over the Rhine to the Schwarzwald in the north and across to the Juras in the west. They stood admiring it for a few minutes. Then they withdrew to a seat and spent a peaceful afternoon, reading.

Hilary proposed taking a tram back to the Rheinweg when they both felt that it was time for coffee and cakes, but Rosamund begged to walk.

"Honestly, Hilary, I feel quite all right now. Besides, I want to buy some picture postcards to send home."

"O.K., but I warn you sending postcards can be a jolly expensive business," Hilary said easily. "I'll send a couple myself. We can write them at the post office."

They easily found a shop, but the choice of card was another matter. Rosamund "swithered", to quote herself, between a dozen different views. Finally, she fixed on one of the Gardens for her parents, one of the Münster for Canon and Mrs. Gay and one of the Rhine for her elder sister, Dorothy. There she had to stop. Apart from the cost of the cards, the postage, unless she was prepared to restrict herself to only five words, would be twenty-five centimes each. Hilary chose her two and they went out to seek the post office, ignoring the fact that they could have posted at the shop.

Hilary knew what to look for, and they soon found the place with a black hunter's horn on a yellow background and the letters P.T.T. which mark all Swiss post offices.

"*You* buy the stamps," Rosamund implored.

Hilary gave her a teasing look. "Oh, don't you think *you* had better do it? It would be a good chance to air your German. I'll tell you what to say."

"No, please! I'd rather not! You do it—oh, please do!"

Hilary laughed. "Funk!" she retorted. "Oh, all right. But you'll have to pull up your socks and learn to speak, Rosamund. You stand over here while I get the stamps."

She left Rosamund by the door and went to the place where they sold stamps. Rosamund drew back out of the way a little and stood looking round with interest. At least a dozen languages sounded all round her, including the national Swiss tongue which is known as Schwyzer-dutch. A serious-looking Swiss girl with fair plaits wound round and round her head hurried in with a pile of parcels. Two Frenchwomen came next, talking excitedly as they went. Rosamund caught a few words and found to her amazement that she understood them.

"Goodness!" she thought to herself. "I *must* be coming on—in French, at any rate! Well, that's something!"

Then Hilary was coming across to her with the stamps and they retired to a table at one side to write the cards. Rosamund finished the one to her parents and the other to the Gays. She was about to address the third to Dorothy when she stopped. Suppose she sent it to Joan? Joan might be pleased to have a view of the Rhine. If it came to that, she might send her one of the Roman remains place on Monday. Rosamund knew that Mary-Lou, Verity and Katharine would probably receive bunches of cards from the other girls, but no one but herself would bother about Joan.

"Finished?" demanded Hilary at that point.

"Just this one to Joan. I shan't be a minute."

She hastily scribbled, "Hope you are having a nice time.

133

This is a lovely place with heaps of interesting things to see. Rosamund." Then they posted the cards and went out into the street where traffic, both wheeled and foot, was going full tilt and the shops were all busy.

"Tram now, I think," Hilary said. "There's a stop farther down. Come along Rosamund. She slipped a hand through Rosamund's arm, for the pavements were thronged. Rosamund looked up at her and smiled happily and Hilary smiled back.

They sauntered along when Rosamund's eye was suddenly caught by a very familiar flash of pink. It was a frock that was the replica of her own. She turned to look across the busy road. The next moment she had jerked her arm from Hilary's hold.

"*Joan!*" she exclaimed.

Before Hilary could collect her wits, she had dashed across the road, and how she escaped being run over was something neither she nor the various furious drivers nor the stunned Hilary was able to say later. She reached the other side in safety, however, and grabbed the arm of the girl in a pink frock like her own and also carrying a week-end case. "Joan! What *are* you doing here? Have you come for the day? I've had to have a tooth out and Hilary stayed with me. She's over there on the other side——"

"Hilary is not!" said a very grim voice behind them. "Hilary is here!"

Still gripping the arm of Joan, who seemed too taken aback by this sudden meeting to do anything but stand still gaping at her, Rosamund swung round to encounter such a glare from Hilary's grey eyes as made her wilt visibly. The next moment the irate prefect had set a hand on a shoulder of each. To Rosamund she seemed to have become inches taller as she stood before them, drawn up to the full extent of her five foot eight.

"And now," said Hilary, still in those grim tones, "I should like to know the meaning of this. Rosamund, why did you rush across the road in that insane way? And you, Joan, what are you doing here when you're supposed to be on the Rösleinalp with Mary-Lou and Verity? What is the meaning of it all?"

CHAPTER XV

HILARY GAINS A VICTORY

THERE was a moment's dead silence during which Rosamund looked fixedly at her shoes and Joan stared straight ahead. At last Rosamund ventured to lift her eyes and murmur, "It was just—I—I—saw Joan."

"Oh, indeed! And was that any valid reason why you should go plunging across the road in that Mad Hatter way? Do you realise that you might have been run over?"

If ever a girl looked idiotic, Rosamund did then.

Hilary turned to Joan. "And why are *you* here, Joan? I know you're alone for Mary-Lou told me they were spending the time on tennis. Do the Careys know you are here?"

"No—and let me alone!" Joan said sullenly. With Hilary standing in the doorway she could hardly make a dash for it. Her only defence lay in being as sulky as she could.

For a moment Hilary was stymied. But she recovered herself quickly. "My dear girl, you can't just go haring off as you like when you're staying with people. What do you think the Careys are feeling? They're responsible for you and they don't know where you are. Mrs. Carey must be crazy with worry about you."

Joan made no reply though she looked rather startled. When the event which had set her off had occurred she had lost both her temper and her head. She had packed her week-end case and gone without caring very much what anyone thought and certainly without troubling about what her hosts might feel.

"We can't stay here," Hilary said at length. "Rosamund, go to the other side of Joan and take her arm. Give me your case, Joan. I'll carry it for you in my free hand." Rosamund clutched one arm and Hilary took the other and she was being marched down the street to a crossing.

"The first thing to do," Hilary was saying, "is to wire the Careys that you are safe. Then—yes; I think we'd

135

better go back to Frau Piguet's and go into all this thoroughly. Post office first, Rosamund."

"I'm not going with you!" Joan exclaimed. "I'm going home on the next train!"

"Have you had bad news?" Hilary demanded.

Joan would not have hesitated to lie if she had thought it would be any use. But she had already told the prefect that the Careys did not know she was here, so there was no hope of her being believed. "No," she proclaimed defiantly. "I'm just going. And I'm not coming back— ever!"

"You're coming with us," Hilary told her calmly. "Please don't start making a scene as if you were a naughty baby expecting to be spanked! Have a little self-respect!"

This touched Joan's pride. She stopped struggling, and the prefect led them over the crossing and back down the street to the post office where she stopped outside and told Rosamund to go and send the wire.

"What shall I say?" Rosamund asked meekly. In the much greater awfulness of Joan's behaviour, her own looked like being forgotten, but she was taking no chances. She knew quite well that it had been mad to rush across the road and Hilary had every reason to be angry.

"Say, 'Joan safe with us in Basle. Will ring up this evening'. Sign it 'Wilmot'," Hilary said. "Miss Wilmot will do the ringing-up, anyhow! Have you money?"

"Oh, yes; plenty!" Rosamund went flying and Hilary concentrated her attention on her prisoner.

"I don't know what's behind all this, Joan," she said gravely, "but you can't possibly go off on a journey like that all alone. You don't speak either French or German and goodness knows what sort of a mess you might get into!"

"I'll manage all right," Joan said furiously. "Let me go! It's no business of yours, so why do you go poking your nose into it? Mind your own affairs and I'll mind mine!"

"It *is* my business," Hilary told her with great calm. "It's the business of any prefect if she sees a younger girl doing a mad thing to stop her."

"Oh, go to hell!" Joan retorted, completely furious.

Hilary eyed her thoughtfully. "I don't know if you *want*

us to think that your people have dragged you up, but you're going the right way about it. Stop using such disgusting language and try to think of your mother a little! You're giving me a nice idea of her!"

It had never dawned on her that her parents would be blamed. She knew very well that if ever her mother had caught her swearing she would have received a sharp slap. Mrs. Baker had never allowed bad language.

Hilary let the conversation lapse, though she was shocked at Joan's remark. They stood in silence until Rosamund, very flushed after wrestling with getting off the telegram, rejoined them. Hilary nodded to her to go to Joan's other side again and then marched them off to the tram stop where they boarded a tram for the garden suburb where Frau Piguet lived. Joan was led up to the top and settled between them. The journey was not a long one, but to her it seemed to last ages. At last Hilary stood up and, at the next stop, they left the tram for the street and were soon at the tall, narrow house where Frau Piguet welcomed them with beaming smiles and the remark that she was glad they had come back.

"We met one of our girls in the city," Hilary said. "Do you mind if she has coffee and cakes with us, Frau Piguet —if it's not too much trouble to give us coffee and cakes."

"Coffee and rolls, these I have always ready. And indeed mein Fräulein, I did not think the poor little one here should be out all day after a so dreadful experience as having a tooth drawn. I will bring the coffee and rolls to the Speisesaal in five short minutes."

Hilary thanked her prettily and she bustled off, while the two girls took Joan up to the dormitory. Hilary left Rosamund and Joan there and ran down again, taking Joan's case with her. She hunted for Frau Piguet and gave it into her charge. She did not *know* that Joan had put her purse in the case, but she guessed at it and felt it would be wiser to be rid of it herself. Surely the girl would have more sense than to try to cross half Europe penniless?

In the dormitory she found Joan standing glowering into space. Rosamund was standing at the door, brushing out her hair. The prefect told her to finish tidying and then run down to the Speisesaal. She herself waited until the younger girl had gone. Then she turned to the sullen Joan.

"Coffee and cakes will be ready in a moment," she said. "I want your solemn word of honour that you won't try to get away until Miss Wilmot has come."

"And suppose I won't give it?" Joan retorted.

"Then I shall lock you in here until she comes." Hilary knew that she was behaving in a very high-handed way, but it seemed to her that high-handedness was the only way to treat Joan. "Either you give me your promise to stay here or I'll lock you in."

"What's it to do with you?" Joan burst out furiously.

"Everything. I'm a prefect and you're a Middle. It's a prefect's job to keep an eye on Middles when there's no mistress to do it. No prefect would allow you to go ramping over Europe alone. I tell you, *it isn't safe!*"

Hilary spoke with such emphasis that Joan was impressed in spite of herself. She was not going to give in without a struggle however. "Oh, raspberries to that!" Her manner was as rude as she could possibly make it. "And don't try to preach to me for I won't listen!"

"I'm not preaching. I'm simply telling you what I'm going to do and why. The choice is yours."

Joan twisted her fingers together. Hilary's quiet self-assurance was having its effect on her. It helped to calm her. She knew that the prefect would keep her word and that if she did not give the promise she would be locked in. Well, she must yield and she must keep her promise. But, oh, if she could ever get even with Hilary Wilson she would!

"Very well," she muttered sulkily. "I'll promise to stay till Miss Wilmot comes. But I hate you, Hilary Wilson! It's no business of yours what I do. And if ever I get a chance to spite you I'll take it! So look out!"

Hilary passed this over. She had sounded very sure of herself, but she had been wondering if she was right if it came to locking Joan in. "Come along down," she said. "Miss Wilmot won't be long now and we can have our coffee in the meanwhile. Follow me!"

She led the way down to the Speisesaal where Rosamund was already sitting at a small table in the window. She looked up as the pair entered. Joan was looking raging mad and Hilary's face was still very bleak. Rosamund decided that it would be wiser to say nothing.

Hilary brought Joan and sat her down on the window side of the table. She herself took the seat next her. The coffee was already there. Frau Piguet had been better than her word, for besides the fancy bread-twists, there were a plate of Basle Leckerli and another of Kugelhopfen, the high, bunlike cakes with hollow centres which were filled with whipped cream. There was a dish of the sweet, ivory butter and another of black cherry jam. Joan had eaten nothing since breakfast at nine o'clock and she was ravenous. She attacked her meal hungrily. Rosamund and Hilary were more moderate and before she took a Kugel-hopf Rosamund looked doubtfully at Hilary.

"Ought I?" she asked.

Hilary was recovering her temper. "How does your tooth feel?" she asked.

Rosamund giggled suddenly. "Not at all. I've absolutely forgotten about it." She delicately tongued the hollow where it had been. "It feels all right."

"Then I don't see why you shouldn't," Hilary replied.

Rosamund risked it and got away with it. Herr Braunen had done a good job of work and she was herself again, though she would be even better after a night's rest. Hilary pressed the cakes on Joan who took one and enjoyed it. She had never tasted anything like it before.

Hilary talked at length and kept the meal a leisurely one. She wanted to spin it out as long as possible. But there are limits to everything and finally they had to rise from the table and let Miggi clear and then lay the tables for Abendessen. Hilary wondered what they could do. She did not dare to take the two for a walk. She had an idea that Joan's promise would hold good only as long as they were in the house. She had seen a gleam in the younger girl's eyes when Rosamund suggested a walk and somehow she meant to keep Joan with them until she could hand the whole thing over to Miss Wilmot.

"And 'glad' doesn't express what I'll feel when I see her!" she thought. "What on earth shall I do with them?"

Then it occurred to her to try to find out why Joan had run away. "Let's go out into the garden," she said.

The garden was a tiny patch where Frau Piguet grew gay annuals in the narrow borders round the small grass plot. It faced south, so got sun most of the day, but now the sun had moved round to the west and it was cool and shadowy. Hilary led the way to a quaint wooden seat and they sat down.

"It's nice and cool here," Rosamund said. "What an awfully hot day it's been!"

"You get that over here," Hilary informed her. "We have deep snow and hard frost in the winter, but the summers are blazing hot. Oh, well, we start swimming and boating next week, so that's so much to the good."

"I'm looking forward to it," Rosamund said. She was speaking very meekly for she could not forget the glare that Hilary had given her that afternoon. Rosamund was going to do nothing to revive the memory!

Hilary turned to Joan. "Do you swim or row?"

"Not me!" Joan growled. "Lot of bosh!"

"Oh, it isn't!" Rosamund cried. "Swimming is good fun, anyhow. I'm looking forward to it."

"You can have it! It won't affect me! I shan't be here!"

Hilary leaned forward. "What's happened, Joan? Can't you tell us? We might be able to put things right."

"Not your business!" Joan growled. "It's *my* affair. Don't be so nosey!"

Hilary flushed with indignation and disgust. Rosamund forgot her caution and broke in. "Oh, Joan! Don't talk such rot! Hilary only wants to help!"

"Then she can keep her help to herself! Anyhow, I'm not staying here with a lot of beastly snobs! Don't you go trying to come the good little girl over me, Ros Lilley! You're nobody! Your ma was only someone's servant——"

She got no further. Hilary, suddenly looking completely grown-up, swung round on her. "That will do! However bad a temper you are in there's no need to be vulgar! Rosamund, didn't you say your father was a gardener? Then you ought to know something about it. Come and tell me what some of these flowers I don't know are. That mauvey thing, for instance? It's awfully pretty."

They walked away, Hilary secure in the knowledge that Joan was unlikely to depart without her case. But Rosamund had time to name only a few of the flowers before the clatter of feet and sound of voices told the prefect that her ordeal was at an end. Miss Wilmot and the others had got back at last. She knew that the girls would go straight upstairs. She decided to stay in the garden with Joan and send Rosamund for the mistress.

"Run and bring Miss Wilmot here, Rosamund," she said urgently. "Don't say anything about Joan, though. Just ask her if she'll come to the garden."

Rosamund was off on the word and Hilary went back to the seat where Joan was still hunched up, mainly occupied in hating everyone. She looked very miserable, and this softened the elder girl's voice as she said, "Miss Wilmot has come back, Joan. I've sent to ask her to come here. But I'll give you one piece of advice. Don't be rude to her. She may be able to straighten things out for you."

Joan gave an inarticulate growl in reply and then there came the sound of light steps and Miss Wilmot, very pretty and fresh-looking in her green cotton frock, arrived.

"Rosamund says you want me, Hilary," she began. Then as Hilary moved forward she saw who was on the seat and her eyes widened. "Joan Baker!" she exclaimed. "What on earth are *you* doing here?"

CHAPTER XVI

MISS ANNERSLEY CUTS THE KNOT

"AND so, you see, I thought the best thing was to bring her to you and let *you* talk to her. *I* can't get her to hear either sense or reason!" Nancy Wilmot sat back in her chair with a sigh of relief. It had been a hectic two days and she was thankful to be rid of the latest responsibility and leave it to Miss Annersley to cope.

The Head looked thoughtful as she listened. It was a sticky position. Then she saw that Nancy was looking at her anxiously and instantly gave the approval for which the young mistress had been hoping.

"It's a very unpleasant business all round and I think you've done the wisest thing, Nancy. And I'm more glad than I can say that Hilary kept her head as she did. When I think that that poor, silly child might have been wandering anywhere, it makes my blood run cold! Thanks to you and Hilary, however, we are spared that."

Nancy Wilmot shrugged her shoulders. "Oh, I imagine she'd have got home all right. As she herself told me last night, she wasn't born yesterday!"

"I daresay! At less than fifteen, I would trust no girl to that limit—most of all a girl like Joan Baker. Yes; I know we can say that most of this is her own silly fault. She eavesdropped deliberately. But that doesn't alter the fact that she might have run into serious difficulties."

"What are you going to do about it?"

"I'm not going to expel her, if that's what you want to know. Most of the other girls know nothing about all this. I don't think either Hilary or Rosamund will talk——"

"They promised me they wouldn't," Nancy interrupted.

"Then we needn't worry about that. It was a stroke of genius to take Joan to Frieda's and get Biddy to take your place with the girls. I'm sorry her holiday had to be broken into, but I'll see that she has a week-end off later on to make up. You're *sure* the others know nothing?"

"Positive! I asked Frau Piguet for the loan of her office and took Joan there and tried to get some sense into her. When I found it was hopeless I left her there with the sketchiest explanation to Frau Piguet. Then, as I told you, I shot them all off to bed early and when they were safely there, ordered a car and took Joan to Frieda's. Thank goodness Frieda is an Old Girl herself and took the whole thing in her stride. And Biddy saw at once that I was right to bring the little wretch straight to you today and agreed at once to take my place. She's telling the girls that sudden school business cropped up and I had to come to see you. And thank goodness even more that you're here in Montreux!" Nancy suddenly relaxed. "Oh, I'm so *tired*! This has been a bit of a strain."

"You poor girl," the Head said, deep sympathy in her

voice. "Well, you can't go back today. You must rest and return tomorrow. In the meantime, I'll see to Joan—with Joey to help," she added as an afterthought.

"I feel a complete pig, unloading a mess like this on you. You need a rest as much as any of us."

"You couldn't do anything else. I'm Head, after all, and the ultimate responsibility is mine. Don't worry about me. I've had an easy two days and I feel fit and ready for anything. Now you go and find the garden and a chair and a nice novel. I'm here, and *I'll* cope."

With this Miss Annersley dismissed her maths mistress firmly and Nancy went to do as she was told. She really did feel tired. She had had a strenuous time sight-seeing, what with the girls and the anxiety about Rosamund's tooth before all the trouble with Joan had broken over her. She found her novel and chair and a shady spot in Mrs. Embury's garden. She found it, but she did little reading. Halfway down the second page, the book fell from her relaxed hold and Nancy slept peacefully

It was the Sunday of half-term and, as she had said, she had heard what Hilary and Rosamund had had to say the previous night after she had swept Joan off to Frau Piguet's quarters out of sight of the others, who knew nothing of what had happened and, if the Head had any say in the matter, never would know. She had sent the two girls to join the others and then rung up the Rösleinalp to relieve Mrs. Carey's mind completely. Neither Mary-Lou nor Katharine could give any explanation of Joan's conduct and Verity Carey knew even less. All they could say was that when they went to the tennis court Commander Carey had rented for the mornings so that the girls might practise, Joan had been *non est*.

At first they had not worried, thinking she had gone off to look at the wood-carvings, lace and embroideries which were displayed in the one shop the place boasted. She had been fascinated by them the day before, and they thought Joan had gone to buy some. But when lunchtime came and she was still missing, they had instituted a thorough search before going home to report. It was almost two o'clock so Mrs. Carey's ordeal of anxiety had not lasted long, for Hilary's wire had arrived before five.

But by that time the Commander had been down to the Görnetz Platz to look for her and Katharine and Mary-Lou had tired themselves out with hunting every corner of the Rösleinalp.

Nancy Wilmot had finally dragged from Joan that the cause of her flight had been "something Mary-Lou and Katharine had said". When she and Joan were safely at the von Ahlens' house she had consulted with Frieda von Ahlen and Biddy O'Ryan, and they had decided that she and Joan should stay the night at the von Ahlens and catch the first train to Montreux next morning to let the Head see what she could do, for Joan had been sullen and refused to say more than she had already said.

It was possible for her to refuse to speak to either gentle Mrs. von Ahlen or the two young mistresses, but she had been unable to hold out against Miss Annersley's steady questioning. In the end she had broken down and admitted that Katharine and Mary-Lou had said nothing to her directly. She had been passing the door of the room the pair were sharing to go to the bathroom that morning and had caught her own name. Curious to hear what they had to say, she had deliberately listened and what she had overheard had roused every worst feeling in her.

"What did they say?" Miss Annersley asked.

"I'm not telling you," Joan muttered.

"I am afraid you must. You see, I must know how far I can excuse such outrageous behaviour as yours. I mean it, Joan. If you won't say, I shall ask Mary-Lou and Katharine and they will tell me. But I shall have to explain *why* I want to know, of course, and I imagine you don't want them to know that you could stoop to such dishonourable and mean tricks."

This had turned the scale. Already Joan knew exactly how the entire Chalet School regarded anything like eavesdropping. Miss Annersley had left her no chance of not knowing. Besides, her anger and pride were dissolving and underneath them still lay the admiration and a certain gratitude she felt for the two girls who had been kind to her. After all Joan was not yet fifteen and there was a good deal of the child in her. She looked at the Head, realised that Miss Annersley meant exactly what she had said, and did the best thing she could have done for herself. She burst into a passion of tears.

Miss Annersley let her cry for a while, knowing that she needed the relief. When the tears threatened to become hysteria, she stopped them firmly, and when Joan was more or less quiet again she repeated her question. "What did they say that made you do such a silly thing?"

"I heard them—they said—said—Mary-Lou said she was—was going to go on being decent to me till I was as decent as—any other Chalet School girl," Joan gasped.

Miss Annersley nearly smiled. She just caught it back in time. But it was so exactly like Mary-Lou! The Head's voice had lost its chilliness as she said, "But what was there about that to send you off like that? Surely it was very kind of Mary-Lou to want to help you to become more like the girls of your school? You must know by this time, Joan, that a lot of the things you say and do are neither said nor done with us. When you are one of a community, life can be very hard if you know that your ideals and standards are lower than those of the rest. For they are, Joan. Make no mistake about that. You think things and say things and do things that none of the others would ever do. Just at first, the girls will make allowances for you, but it won't go on."

"I'm not worse than the others,' Joan said sulkily.

"Is that quite true, my dear?"

Joan reddened, but she had no reply to make. She might pretend to think that honourable conduct was fussy and silly, but in her heart she already knew that it was not. Part of her bitterness had been because Rosamund Lilley had not had to learn all this. She already knew it. She had found that the things she had felt so grand about in the old days were disliked and despised by these girls, and she had had nothing to take their place—except her tennis and that did not make up for all.

Miss Annersley waited and presently the culprit looked up. "I—I suppose—but it's all so *different* here! I—before, the girls thought I was someone and—but——"

Joan stopped there for by this time she was so tied up that she was not very sure *what* she wanted to say. Miss Annersley nodded and proceeded to cut the knot.

"In fact," she said gravely, "pride was at the bottom of it all. At your other school a lot of silly girls laughed when you were rude to people and so you began to think you were witty and clever instead of being plain rude! You did things that seemed to them daring and so you thought you *were* daring. You jeered at things that struck you as silly and fussy, and they applauded you and so you thought you were right. Then you came here and found that no one was going to think you either witty or clever or daring and you didn't like it. When one or two girls decided to help you to pull up to what you ought to be, it hurt your pride. That was it, wasn't it, Joan?"

Joan nodded voicelessly. Speech was beyond her.

Miss Annersley suddenly swung to her feet and came to sit beside her, an arm round her shoulders. "Oh, my poor little girl! What a lot of misery you have made for yourself! And what a lot of worry you have given other people. But it's going to be different now, isn't it?"

Joan was crying again, but these tears were different. She felt how foolish she had been and was vowing that if only the Head would give her another chance, she would show them how different she could be. But *would* she? Hadn't she, Joan, sinned beyond forgiveness?

As if she could read the girl's thoughts—perhaps, to a certain extent she could—Miss Annersley spoke again and all the ice had gone from her lovely voice. "Yes, Joan; it's going to be different now. You're going to put all this wrong-doing and silliness behind you and show us what a really nice girl Joan Baker is when she tries."

Joan removed the sopping handkerchief and looked up. "Do you mean you'll forgive me?" she choked.

The Head smiled into the swollen, tear-drenched eyes. "Of course I do. You need have no fear of that, Joan." And she drew the girl closer and kissed her. "Now, you have a long, hard way to tread, I'm afraid, and if it ever seems too hard to you, remember that you've brought most of it on yourself and it is only you who can climb it and only you who can make it easier by not rebelling."

"I'll remember," Joan whispered. She was still shaking from the storm, but already she felt happier than she had done for many a long day.

"You have certain things you must do first," Miss Annersley went on.

Joan started and looked at her. What was coming? The Head smiled at her again. "You won't like them, but they *must* be done. We have to clear all the stumbling-blocks out of your way so that you can go ahead without any pauses. First, you must write a letter of apology to Commander and Mrs. Carey. Oh yes; you must," as she saw the flash in Joan's eyes. "You have been very rude and ill-bred. I'm sure you're sorry for all the worry you caused Mrs. Carey, especially when she has been so ill?" She paused, and Joan nodded. "Well, then, of course you will tell her so. I shall leave what you do about Katharine and Mary-Lou to yourself. They have no idea that you listened to their private conversation. So far as I'm concerned, they never will hear of it."

Joan looked down. At the moment she felt that she could never summon up courage to make such a confession and ask pardon for it. The Head knew that, but she said no more. Miss Annersley hoped that by the end of the term she would have made such strides that she would be able to bring herself to it. She knew the two girls well enough to be sure that if Joan did manage it they would forgive and forget—especially Mary-Lou, who had never yet learned how to hold a grudge against anybody.

"Finally," the Head continued, "you must apologise to Miss Wilmot and Miss O'Ryan for all the trouble you have given them. Miss O'Ryan has had to give up her own holiday and take charge of the others while Miss Wilmot brought you here. All this is *your* fault, Joan, and you owe both mistresses an apology."

It was a bitter pill to swallow. From babyhood Joan had loathed saying she was sorry. Latterly she had never bothered to do it. But she was in earnest when she had told Miss Annersley that she would try. She gulped hard.

"I'll—I'll do it. I—I am sorry. And—I've spoilt *your* holiday too. Please, I'm very sorry about that too."

"If you can go on that way," Miss Annersley said quietly, "you will succeed. But don't think it'll all be plain sailing. You've given way to the demon of pride for a long time now, and you can't expect to slay him when

147

you've only just put on your uniform. But remember this. Every time you defeat him, it comes just a shade easier next time. Every time you surrender, you are making it just that much harder for yourself next time. And now, you are very tired and I expect your head is aching after all the crying you've done. You may go upstairs and take off your frock and sandals and lie down on your bed and try to sleep it off. Just one last thing, Joan. The fight must be yours, but we are never left to stand alone. Help is ours if we ask for it. Remember that when you say your prayers, night and morning, and ask that help may be given you always to conquer your bosom foe. Prayer is the mightiest weapon we have, and if we'll only use it we'll come out victors in the end."

She dismissed Joan after that—a very subdued and penitent Joan. When she went up to the little room an hour later it was to find the girl asleep, and she nodded to Joey Maynard who was at the door, her baby in her arms.

"All well?" Joey murmured in a low tone, that she had learned years ago at school was less likely to disturb sleepers than a whisper.

"All well!" Miss Annersley gently brushed the loose hair back from the flushed face. Then she came out of the room and removed Baby Cecil from her mother.

"Give me my newest future pupil. Oh, if only parents would realise how much their children's happiness depends on careful training from babyhood onwards, what a lot of trouble everyone would be saved!"

"That's true," Joey said as they went down to the drawing-room where Miss Annersley sat cuddling Cecil joyfully. "All the same, Hilda, all the careful training in the world can't always counteract original sin. Look what we've had to go through with young Margot!"

"I know. But it has held all through. Margot has listened to her devil, over and over again, but there have been times when she has turned her back on him, and now that she is older and more sensible she is really putting up a big fight. And she's had you and Jack and your teaching behind her and she's turning into a thoroughly nice girl. But Joan has a long way to go and she has none of the props you've given Margot. She's in for a bad time, poor child. I only hope this silly affair has given her such a shock that she never goes back. At least we must see to it that no carelessness on our part helps her backwards."

Joey gave her a queer look. "I shouldn't worry. You've done your part faithfully enough this morning or I don't know you. I think Joan will try."

"I agree!" Miss Wilmot had awakened and come to see if lunch was to the fore. She had overheard her Head's last speech and Joey's reply. "You've won, then? Good for you! It was beyond me, but I thought you'd do it! Joan will buck up now and who knows, we may yet see her the joy and pride of our declining years!"

"I'd love to know how you solved the problem, Hilda, but it isn't fair to ask," said Joey. "Besides," with a wicked grin, "I can guess. You ticked me off often enough for the good of my soul when *I* was a kid at school. See what a model of all the virtues I've become, thanks to Hilda's training—or in part, anyway. You'd better be looking for a halo to fit me!" and she escaped to the hall, followed by Nancy's retort, "It isn't a halo you need, my good woman. It's a new hat ten sizes larger than usual!"

CHAPTER XVII

JOAN MAKES FULL AMENDS

IT was the last full day of term. Exams were over. The garden party with which the school generally closed the summer term lay behind them, having taken place the day before and been a great success. The Matrons were finishing up the packing. There was really nothing left to do now, but put in the few hours left before the school scattered for the next eight weeks.

"Have a doubles with Katt and Blossom and me?" Mary-Lou invited Carola Johnstone when the afternoon rest period was over. "I put down our names for Court A. Not if you don't want to, but I'd rather like it to be you."

Carola, who had been looking very serious, nodded. "I'd love it—my last game at school, worse luck!"

"I think you're an ass not to come back for a last year at St. Mildred's," Katharine remarked.

"I'd have liked it, but Dad's off to Samoa on some new germ-hunt and he wants Mother and me with him," Carola replied. "And, after all, I'm past seventeen now. I've got to wait till I'm eighteen before I can go to Bedford, and I may as well have the fun of a trip to the South Seas."

Blossom Willoughby laughed. "I wonder if you'll come across the Ozanne twins? They're sculling about there somewhere. Give them my love if you ever do."

"Not very likely. The South Sea islands are quite a few hundred miles apart," Carola told her gravely. Then she broke into laughter. "That's more or less what Vi Lucy and Barbara Chester said when they heard where I was going. You people never learn much geography."

"Samoa? That's where Robert Louis Stevenson is buried," Mary-Lou said thoughtfully. "Mind you go and see his grave, Carola, and give him a hail for me. I've admired him awfully since I read his life."

"You'll have to send us postcards and long letters describing the place," put in Katharine.

"I thought you were born out there?" Blossom said, giving further proof of her ignorance of geography.

"No; in Singapore. *That's* not the South Seas."

"Isn't it? I quite thought it was."

"However you got into any Sixth form is beyond me!" Katharine exclaimed. "Do you know *nothing*, Blossom?"

Blossom grinned. "It was a scrape, I admit. But my English carried me through."

"It's as well you won't have to earn your own living," Mary-Lou retorted as they reached the court. "I don't know what you'd have done, for they demand degrees or diplomas for most things nowadays."

"Oh, been a mannequin or gone charring," Blossom said with her usual insouciance. "I'll have plenty to do at home anyhow. Mummy is very tied with Aubrey and Baby, and I know she expects me to give her a hand."

The girls said no more. They knew that Blossom's younger brother, little Aubrey, was very frail and the year-old baby who had come to round out the family was one person's work at any time. Mary-Lou suggested they should call for side and service and Katharine looked round to see if any Juniors were on hand to act as ball-boys. None were, but Rosamund Lilley and Len Maynard came on the scene and volunteered without being asked.

"Sure you don't mind?" the Games prefect asked.

"Rather not!" Len said. "Besides, it's the last chance we'll have of doing it for Carola. Why aren't you going on to St. Mildred's, Carola?"

"Because I'm going to Samoa instead," Carola returned impatiently. "And I wish you people wouldn't talk as if I were saying good-bye for ever! It's only for a year until I go to Bedford and once there I expect I'll be hopping over to Switzerland often. Now dry up!"

Rosamund laughed. "I thought Switzerland sounded like the far end of the world when Mrs. Gay offered her scholarship and I knew I'd won it. Samoa sounds to me like going to another planet!"

Katharine and Mary-Lou exchanged glances, unseen by the others. Whatever else had happened that term, Rosamund had become completely reconciled to being at the Chalet School.

"In fact," Mary-Lou said when they talked it over afterwards, "she's well on the way to being a thoroughly representative Chalet girl! Oh, I don't say she'll ever make a big stir unless she comes out as a writer. She might, you know. That article of hers in the *Chaletian* on famous gardens was quite good for a kid."

They stopped talking and set to on a fierce doubles which was won by Mary-Lou and Katharine. By the time it ended a number of the Middles were there, watching, and rounds of applause rang out as the victors shook hands with their opponents.

Joan had been among them. This second half of the term had been different for her. It had, as the Head had shrewdly foreseen, been a very hard time for her. She had so much to get rid of and so much to learn that it was with difficulty she made headway at all. Over and over again she had only just saved herself from some piece of impertinence. She *had* got into serious trouble with Carola when she had cheeked the prefect outrageously on being told to put her books away tidily at the end of prep.

Carola, who never stood any nonsense, had told her exactly what she was, and by the time it was over Joan was feeling like crawling under the nearest desk and staying there. But if Carola had what the Scots call "an illscrapit tongue", she easily forgave and forgot, and when Joan had finally begged her pardon it was done with.

But for all she had gained so far, Joan had never yet succeeded in bringing herself to owning up to Katharine and Mary-Lou how she had deliberately listened to a very private conversation of theirs. Once or twice she had made up her mind to do it, but when it came to the point, she shrank from it. And though she *had* apologised to both Mrs. Carey and Mary-Lou for going off as she had at half-term, the worst part of the business remained a mystery to the Rösleinalp party.

Now, as they all streamed back to school to see about Kaffee und Kuchen, she had those qualms again about going on like this and still not owning up. But to confess in cold blood that she had stood outside the door to listen! No; it was more than she could manage!

If she had but known it, help was coming to her from a totally unexpected direction. Joey Maynard had returned to Freudesheim some weeks before this. Winifred Embury had come home safely from the hospital to convalesce after her operation and Joey had joyfully flown home to pick up the reins there. Cecil showed every sign of becoming an obstreperous young person, even at three months, and Joey felt that it was easier to deal with her in her own nursery. However, the young lady was beginning to learn that "No" meant "No", and Mrs. Maynard decided that she could spare an hour or two to say goodbye to the girls before they parted for the holidays. Besides, she had been in the thick of all the half-term trouble and she wanted to know how it was working out. She came across after she had put Cecil to bed and kissed the twins good-night in their cots.

She arrived in the garden just as the girls were gathering for rambles and made a bee-line for Joan who was standing with Rosamund and the triplets. The latter flung themselves on their mother with enthusiasm.

"Mamma, oh, Mamma! It's so nice to have you home!" Con exclaimed.

"*We'll* be home tomorrow," Margot added. "Where's Cecil? We'd all have loved to see her."

"Cecil is in bed and asleep as you ought to know," her mother said. "As for being at home, *that* isn't going to last very long."

"Why not?" they all cried together.

"Because, my lambs, we're going away these holidays. First we're going to spend a week with Tante Simone and Oncle André to see *her* new baby and show them Cecil. Then we're going home to Plas Gwyn for a month.[1] The new Rectory has been built and Gwensi and her brother are moving in there in September, so Papa and I have to decide what to do about the house. We are thinking of letting it, and in that case, we've got to do something about all our things that are still there."

"What about Emmy?" Margot demanded. Emerence Hope had been invited to spend the summer holidays with the Maynards.

"Emmy will come with us, of course. And we have to pop down to the Quadrant to see all the family there and Auntie Madge will want us at *their* new house." She turned as Miss O'Ryan came to claim the five for her ramble and said, "Are you being responsible for this lot, may I ask? You are? Then be a gem and let me keep Joan Baker, will you? I did see Rosamund at the beginning of term and I'll have a word with her now if you can wait long enough. Then I'd like to take Joan over to Freudesheim for a short time. She doesn't know me properly and I can't have that. Can't have any Chalet School girl who doesn't know me!"

Biddy laughed. "Sure, you'll go on coaxing till I agree so I may as well do it at once. Very well. Have your word with Rosamund and then, Joan, you may go with Mrs. Maynard. She'll return you in time for Abendessen. You three, go and get your hats and, Rosamund, fetch yours when Mrs. Maynard has finished with you."

[1] Joey Goes to the Oberland.

The triplets raced off and Joey slipped a slender hand through Rosamund's arm. "Well? How about it? Are you happy here now? Wasn't I right when I told you that no one here would care who or what your people were so long as you were nice yourself?" she demanded.

Rosamund looked up and laughed. "Oh, a million times right! It's the best thing that ever happened to me that Canon and Mrs. Gay gave me their scholarship! And the girls know all about Mum and Dad and it hasn't made a scrap of difference to them."

"And you're happy?" Joey asked insistently.

"Awfully happy! I love the school and I'm glad I came."

"Then that's all right! Now I mustn't keep you, or Miss O'Ryan will be talking to me! Good-bye, Rosamund. Have you heard anything about removes yet?"

"No; the Head said she'd tell us that next term. But I'm *eating* up French now—I can even talk a little. And I'm not too bad in German either. I'm ninth in form order and eleventh in exams, so that isn't too bad."

"It's extremely good when you had to learn two new languages straight off the reel," Joey said heartily. "Good for you, Rosamund! Now you must go! Good hunting!"

"That's from *The Jungle Books*?" Rosamund queried. "Thank you, Mrs. Maynard. Good hunting to you!" Then she had to run because the rest had formed into line for the march down the road.

Joey waved to them and then turned to Joan. "Come along, Joan. We'll go to my house and have a good talk there." She took Joan's arm and turned her in the direction of the dividing hedge. "We'll go through the gardens. Do you realise that you've been here practically a whole term and I still don't know you? Except for the year we were in Canada, I don't think such a thing has ever happened before in the annals of the Chalet School."

Joan looked at her shyly. She really knew Joey by sight only. That lady might claim to have been in the midst of the half-term fuss, but actually, she had kept out of it at the time. The only thing of which she had no idea was the eavesdropping, and not even to her had the Head breathed a word of that unpleasant affair.

"Well," Joey said, when they were established in her

charming Saal and Anna had been asked for lemonade and cakes, "and how do you like the school now you've had a real chance to sample it?"

"I—like it," Joan said.

"Good! Did you ever hear how it all began—oh, thank you, Anna! Just pop it down and then you'd better go for a stroll. You haven't been out all day." And Joey smiled affectionately at the sturdy Tirolean who had been her mainstay ever since her marriage.

"Danke, meine Dame," Anna said, giving her mistress a look of pure adoration before she left the room.

Joey poured out lemonade for them both, handed Joan a glass and the plate of cakes and then continued her speech placidly. "Has anyone told you how we began? [1] It was years ago, when I was a kid, younger than you. I was a nuisance in those days—took a cold if it came within a mile of me. We'd been left horridly poor and my sister—that's your Madame—had to think of something to do. We knew Tirol pretty well, having spent two or three holidays on the Tiern See, and she decided that she would try to have a school for girls up there. She began with me and one other girl, Grizel Cochrane, who used to teach music at the school. She's running a music shop with another Old Girl in New Zealand now.

"Well, we grew almost at once and went on growing. Then Sir James Russell—he was only Dr. Jem in those days—opened a Sanatorium up on the Sonnalpe, which is on the opposite side of the lake. That meant that we got a great many more and so it's gone on. We've had our ups and downs, but you'll have to ask the others about those. Just now, I'll wind up by saying that now we are back in the Alps again, though we still have an English branch, and we all hope we'll be able to stay here as long as the school is in existence. Potted history!" she added laughing.

"It sounds thrilling," Joan said with a smile.

"Yes; I've had a few hectic adventures in my time," her hostess agreed, watching her. Joan had smiled, but there was a shadow at the back of her eyes and Joey meant to know why before she let the girl go back to school. She pressed another of the delicious little cakes,

[1] The School at the Chalet.

all honey and nuts, which were a speciality of Anna's on her and then changed the subject.

"How are you getting on with French and German?"

"French only poor, but German is easier," Joan replied.

Joey chuckled. "Not like Rosamund then. She says she can even talk a little in French, but I gather the German is still a bit sticky."

She went on with her cheerful chatter for the next twenty minutes or so, but she was watching Joan all the time and she knew that all was not well with the girl.

"I'm clearing that away before she goes home or my name's not Josephine Mary Maynard!" Joey vowed inwardly. She had given Joan several openings, but the girl seemed disinclined to take them. Evidently a frontal attack must be made and she promptly made it. "Joan, what's wrong with you? Now don't start in saying there's nothing wrong. You don't suppose after all my experience of girls I don't know when one is feeling miserable deep down under everything, do you? What is it? Tell me and perhaps I can help you out. I will if I can."

Joan jumped, nearly upsetting her glass, and went darkly red. Joey caught the glass before it overturned completely, and then repeated her query, "What is it?"

Up till this time Joan had felt that she could never tell anyone what she had done, but now, with those black eyes, soft as pansies, looking at her and that golden voice asking her what was wrong and offering help, all her defences suddenly went down. She tumbled off her chair on to the floor and knelt at Mrs. Maynard's knee and hid her face in her lap. Joey set aside her own glass and stroked the wiry hair from which the "perm" was growing out.

"Tell me," she said softly. "If there's anything badly wrong, you can't be really happy, no matter what happens. I'll help you to put it right. What have you done—cheated at lessons? Helped yourself to someone else's sweets or pencils? What is it, Joan?"

"Oh, it's worse than that! You'll never want anything more to do with me when you hear!" Joan gasped.

"Rubbish! What do you think I am—an angel? Not very likely!" quoth Joey. "My dear girl, we all have things in our lives that make us feel bitterly ashamed. We can't undo them, more's the pity, but we can own up and ask for forgiveness and make up our minds to try not to do them again. Then we have to keep on trying. And that is all the very greatest saint that ever lived can do. Tell me what it is and we'll work it out together."

Joan caught her breath. Then—it all came out. Joey listened to her halting confession in silence, but there was nothing chilling in her silence. Joan could feel warm sympathy and pity and it made everything easier.

"Miss Annersley knows, but she said she wouldn't tell anyone else, not even Mary-Lou and Katharine," she ended. "I *want* to tell them. They've been so decent to me, even after the way I behaved, and I feel such a pig not owning up, but I simply *can't*! I've tried and I can't!"

"Oh, but I think you can," Joey told her. "In fact, you're going to do it now—or as soon as I can get those two over here. Have some more lemonade and take another cake while I go and ring up, and while we wait for them I'll take you up to the night nursery and let you have a dekko at my babies. Do you like babies, Joan?"

"I don't know. I never had much to do with them, only Pam, my kid sister. Mrs. Maynard, don't you loathe and despise me, now you know?" And Joan raised her head and met Joey's eyes at last.

"Not in the least. I loathe and despise what you *did*. It was dishonest and dishonourable. But your sin isn't *you*. Who am I to loathe and despise anyone who does a thing like that? If I'd ever been tempted that way, I might have done the same myself. And," she added, "you'll find that both Mary-Lou and Katharine will feel the same way—especially Mary-Lou."

She refilled Joan's glass, pushed the cakes towards her and went to ring up the school. The prefects together with some of Va had not gone far in their ramble, and Rosalie Dene offered to see if she could find the two Joey wanted and send them across.

"Tell them to stir their stumps!" Joey ordered.

She went back to the Saal to find Joan dabbing her eyes with a handkerchief, but took no more notice than to say, "They're coming! Now come on and see our youngest hopes—but for mercy's sake go quietly. I don't want them roused up."

A peep at the twins and Cecil proved very refreshing, and when they returned to the Saal Mary-Lou and Katharine were sitting there, eyeing the plate of cakes hungrily. Joey pushed Joan towards them.

"Joan has something to own up to you two," she said. "I'll leave you to it while I hunt up some more cakes and glasses. Get on with it, Joan." Joey then left the room.

Meanwhile Joan, thrust into it, gasped and then stammered, "I—I listened at the door to you two talking—when I ran away. I heard what you said. I stood there and listened on purpose. C-can you forgive me?"

The pair looked swiftly at each other. Then Mary-Lou took the initial step. "Forgive you? Of course we can! Is *this* why you've been going round looking such a Peter Grievous all this half-term? Oh, Joan, what an *ass* you've been! Why on earth didn't you tell us right away? Now that's that and we'll never even think of it again, so buck up and let's see a grin on your face for a change!"

But Katharine was older than Mary-Lou. She came to Joan, holding out her hand. "We'll forgive you, of course, just as Mary-Lou says. I won't say don't think of it again, Joan. I think you'll want to think of it when you're tempted again and let it help you to stand back. But don't be unhappy about it any more. And I think you've been awfully plucky to own up after all this time," she added. "That took some doing, I know."

They sat down after that, and Mary-Lou calmly handed round the cakes. "We'll have to wait for the lemonade till Aunt Joey gets back, but there's no reason why we shouldn't sample Anna's best while we're waiting."

And that was all that was ever said about it. But it sent Joan home next day a much happier girl. It also sent her home determined to do her best to become what Mary-Lou called "a *real* Chalet School girl". It had been a difficult problem for everyone, but it was solved at last, and the school had two more people in it who would some day go out into the world and make it just that much happier and better because of the Chalet School way of thinking and doing.

The Nancy Drew Mystery Stories
by Carolyn Keene

Don't miss the latest exciting adventures in this action-packed series!

The Secret in the Old Lace (53)
A strange mystery from the past takes Nancy to Belgium in search of fabulous treasure. But a secret enemy lurks in the winding streets – an enemy who is determined to destroy her . . .

Coming soon

The Greek Symbol Mystery (54)
Nancy's life is in danger when she goes to Greece on the trail of a ruthless gang of art smugglers. Will she manage to outwit her enemies, or will the riddle of the ancient Byzantine mask remain unsolved for ever . . . ?

Armada

CAPTAIN ARMADA

has a whole shipload of exciting books for you

Here are just some of the best-selling titles that Armada has to offer:

- The Palomino Mystery Ann Sheldon 90p
- The Millionaire's Handbook Peter Eldin 85p
- The Mystery of Smugglers Cove Franklin W. Dixon 85p
- Calculator Fun and Games Ben Hamilton 85p
- Pony Puzzles Charlotte Popescu 80p
- The Mystery of the Moss-Covered Mansion Carolyn Keene 85p
- Mill Green on Fire Alison Prince 85p
- Biggles, Pioneer Air Fighter Capt. W. E. Johns 90p
- 5th Armada Crossword Book Robert Newton 85p
- Mystery Stories Enid Blyton 85p

Armadas are available in bookshops and newsagents, but can also be ordered by post.

HOW TO ORDER
ARMADA BOOKS, Cash Sales Dept., GPO Box 29, Douglas, Isle of Man, British Isles. Please send purchase price of book plus postage, as follows:—

     1—4 Books .... 10p per copy
     5 Books or more .... no further charge
     25 Books sent post free within U.K.

Overseas Customers: 12p per copy

NAME (Block letters)

ADDRESS
